D1036594

SANTIAGO

At the age of three he'd lost his father and when he was five his mother married Lieutenant Hennessy, leaving him with his grandparents. Santiago was the name Rudi Thorne had chosen for himself. After wandering lonesome for some years, he became involved in a scheme to run guns into Mexico and met a lot more trouble than he'd bargained for. A surprise meeting was to bring him full circle and he met death every step of the way.

Books by Amy Sadler
in the Linford Western Library:

A MAN OF TEXAS
THE SONS OF BATT COLTRAIN
LUCK IS WHERE YOU FIND IT

AMY SADLER

---◆---

SANTIAGO

Complete and Unabridged

LINFORD
Leicester

First published in Great Britain in 1997 by
Robert Hale Limited
London

First Linford Edition
published 1998
by arrangement with
Robert Hale Limited
London

British Library CIP Data

Sadler, Amy
    Santiago.—Large print ed.—
    Linford western library
    1. Western stories
    2. Large type books
    I. Title
    823.9′14 [F]

    ISBN 0–7089–5205–4

Published by
F. A. Thorpe (Publishing) Ltd.
Anstey, Leicestershire

Set by Words & Graphics Ltd.
Anstey, Leicestershire
Printed and bound in Great Britain by
T. J. International Ltd., Padstow, Cornwall

This book is printed on acid-free paper

1

T HE horse stumbled and the rider yanked up its head. It was almost a week since Thorne had come down out of the lower Sierra Madre and he was hoping that soon he would cross the Rio Grande and into El Paso where he would rest up awhile. Both he and his horse were travel weary. It would be good to soak his body in a tub of hot water — his crotch felt as if a thousand fleas had taken residence there. For days he had seen no one and felt only the hot wind at his back. Yet, Thorne knew he travelled this wild lonely land with others. At night he'd heard the scuffling sounds of tiny feet and the sudden death scream of some desert creature. He knew he must be ever alert. There might be Apaches, bandits, and probably Federales almost

1

anywhere. He urged Single onwards, his eyes always searching the scene.

Thorne slid back his hand to the knife hanging at his belt and unbuttoned the flap of the scabbard as he saw Single's ears swing backwards then forwards and the horse moved faster.

The Indian came swiftly without a sound from behind a boulder and in one leap was on to the horse's rump. Thorne pulled the knife and slashed backwards into the brave's side. He let out a yell. Single went up as he felt the heels sink into his side and the reins yank his head. The Indian slid off to the ground. Swinging Single across the track Thorne moved in behind some boulders and got down; taking his rifle from the saddle scabbard he looked through a gap. He could see three more Apaches, two riding and one running up the trail. He fired two shots and stopped the runner in his stride and he lay prone. The other two turned their paint horses into a crevice on the rough slope. Thorne's first attacker had gone across the trail to take cover leaving a trail of blood spots in the dust.

There might be more of them Thorne thought as he replaced the two spent shells. Perhaps there were others waiting for him up ahead. He was angry at himself for not having noticed he was riding into a short passage which was ideal for an ambush. If he ran for it he doubted the cayuses could outrun Single, but the horse and he were tired, or he'd make a try for it. He'd slept but two hours last night and not much before that for days.

A stone rattled almost opposite and he caught a brief sight of an Apache going up amongst the rocks and scrub. Could it be there were only the three? He looked around him and saw he had good back cover as the land went up about 600 feet. For the moment he was all right.

A shot rang out echoing around the rocks and Single jumped but he stayed close in to the bank. It was probably the horse the Apaches were after, unless they were on the warpath. Usually they didn't bother riders such as Thorne. Over the past years he had often sat and parleyed with Indians and shared his tobacco. Apaches were another breed though, and if they took the notion to kill one they'd do just that. Well, he wasn't ready to die at twenty-seven. Especially the way they might choose to kill him. A bullet sent chippings off a boulder to his left. Another shot plunked into the bank to his right, above. Suddenly there was a whoop and an Apache came straight for his hiding place. In one bound he was atop the boulder and Thorne shot him with his side-arm through the chest before he came down landing right on him, forcing Thorne up against the horse. It snorted and pranced. Thorne got a hand at the Apache's throat and squeezed. He put a leg behind the Indian forcing him to bend. Suddenly the Indian's grip went limp and he fell sideways. Thorne put

4

another bullet into him quickly.

The horse snorted again and backed up as the one Thorne had knifed came at him. He could see the blood oozing through a piece of dirty cloth tied at the Apache's waistline. The fiery fierce brave came at him wielding a knife and Thorne lifted the Winchester off the ground and whacked it down hard on the knife arm. He heard the bone crack, saw the look of pain in the eyes, as the Apache gasped. Still he came on. Thorne had to admire his grit. He swung the rifle again, this time hitting across the windpipe and the Apache fell. As he was about to smash in his head with the rifle butt he felt a load on his back. He rammed back hard against the boulder with considerable force and got a hold on the Apache's long hair yanking him over. The brave was thrown and lay stretched in front of Thorne who kicked him hard in the crotch then stamped on his arm holding a tomahawk before the Indian could move. Thorne was a tall, lean, broad-shouldered man with plenty of strength. He had laid out quite a few larger men than he in his time out here in the West. He lifted up the Indian by the front of the old faded army shirt he wore over nankeen pants, and punched him hard, then swung him round and taking hold of his head jerked it sharply round and broke his neck, and dropped him next to the other two.

Thorne was sweating hard as he took the canteen from the pommel and swallowed some of the brackish water he'd filled it with at the last water-hole. The horse nickered and he gave it a handful. "Best we be careful, old boy, we can't be sure when we'll get more," he told Single.

Thorne went and looked for the two Indian ponies and after finding them behind some rocks, he slipped the rope bridles off them, took the blankets, then slapped them hard on the rump and they ran off back the way they had come. He then dragged the one he had first shot and put him with the others and spread the blankets over them. He quickly got mounted and an hour later he was riding wearily through the undulating scrubland. At the top of a rise he stopped and taking out his field-glasses he surveyed the scene. Way up ahead he could see a few adobes. There, he reckoned he would find water, and food.

Arturo Santos saw the rider coming. The horse, he saw, walked like it had travelled far, and the rider was sagging a little in the saddle and had dust on him. A big gringo, he smiled. Santos hoped he would have plenty of *dinero* on him. Business had not been good of late. One of these days he would move to a more lucrative place. He called to the woman who sat in the shade of a cholla, fanning herself. It was 120° and was only ten o'clock.

Thorne rode up to the run-down adobe which had Cantina, barely visible, written on it. He swung down and his legs sagged slightly as his feet hit the hard ground.

"You come *mucho* the long way, *señor?*" Thorne heard a voice ask him.

"*Si*, I need *agua* and *comida*, the *caballo* also," Thorne told the emaciated-looking Mexican who came forward and took the reins. "Go in, *señor*, I look after the *caballo*," Santos told him.

Thorne went in and sank on to a hard bench at a rough table, his back to the wall from where he could see the open doorway. This he did from habit. Once he had been caught leaning on a bar near a door and two trail bums had walked in and put a gun in his ribs and taken his wallet. Fortunately, he kept only a little in his wallet, the rest inside his inner hat band, though he never carried a great deal of money, unless he had reason to. Today he had on him a cheque for $10,000 for the guns he had delivered to a certain Peter Varig, $2,000 of which would be his when he got to the bank in El Paso.

The rather jaded-looking Mexican

woman brought tacos and a bowl of chilli. Thank God this would be the last of this stomach-rotting muck, Thorne thought. After he had swallowed two tequilas and sat smoking a thin cheroot, he could hardly keep his eyes open. As Santos came in, the woman came over and took the bowl away. Santos came and sat down opposite Thorne. "You stay the night, *señor*? I got a room, one dollar with breakfast, and fifty cents for the chilli, the same for the *caballo*," he informed Thorne.

"I think I'd better," said Thorne. "You wake me at sun-up." He put two dollars on to the table, and an extra two bits. "Give the horse some grain if you have it," he added.

"Si, *señor*. This I do!"

Thorne went outside and sluiced his face off in a bowl of water the woman provided, then after he'd relieved himself by a corral full of goats and sheep, he went back inside. He observed three men who now sat eating chilli noisily. They regarded him from under their sombreros with curiosity as Maria Santos led him through to the rear where Thorne stepped around an assortment of sacks full of dried goods in a short passage that led to the room. Maria lit the lamp that stood on a table, over which a crucifix hung. There was just the small narrow bed and one chair, and a curtain to draw across the doorway. Well, it was better than sleeping in a dry wash with one eye open for Apaches or bandits, Thorne thought.

The woman paused in the doorway. "If you need anything more, *señor* . . . ?"

"*Nada*," Thorne said hurriedly. He'd heard the three devious-looking Mexicans' remarks about Maria, how she would be taking care of the gringo, as he'd left the cantina. Even had he been feeling the need, he'd never fancied heavily bosomed women, and in his present unkempt state he would have been reluctant, had Maria been a nice young attractive female. He got out of his outer clothing after drawing the curtain over the doorway and placing his side-gun, his hat and wallet next to the wall by his pillow, he got under the blanket. A few minutes later he was into deep sleep.

The sky was just showing a hint of yellow when the woman shook him awake. She lit the lamp as he sat up yawning. "You sleep good?" she asked him.

"I guess I must have," Thorne replied.

"You like the eggs and coffee, *señor*?" Maria asked.

"Sounds good," said Thorne.

When he went through there was a real breakfast aroma. The eggs were scrambled and there was bread. The coffee wasn't too bad either. Of Santos there was no sign. After he was ready to leave he found Single under a lean-to and he got saddled up. The dawn was breaking on another hot day to come. A cockerel crowed and sheep were baa-ing way off somewhere. Before he left Thorne emptied his pocket of some pesos. "Here, you might as well have these," he said dropping them into Maria Santos' hand. She smiled broadly. "*Muchas gracias, señor. Vaya con Dios*," she called as he swung into the saddle.

It was as he sat at the top of a long rise that Thorne, looking through his field-glasses across a long stretch of land before he would come to the river, thought he saw riders in the scrub. Well, he ought to make the river before long. He would not cross until it was dark. A rider could easily be picked off mid-stream, he was thinking. He did not wish to announce his arrival into town by taking the usual way in over the bridge. The Rurales might decide to check him out. They could be very awkward when they wanted to. If they saw the cheque they might decide to throw him in jail and . . . Thorne shuddered. Well, it was the last time; he had finished doing favours. Running guns was a dangerous game, especially in Mexico. One never knew who was in office. None of them was to be trusted. Things changed daily. Life was cheap down here.

Thorne stiffened as something glinted way over near the trail which he had left an hour ago after seeing the fresh tracks of three horses. Last evening those three Mexicans had looked him over. He swung the glasses. Way down below in a hollow he could see three horses. Two men sat by some rocks, another lay on top of a boulder. It was obvious they were waiting for someone, something. Was it himself? Whether or not they were those three, he couldn't tell. He swung the glasses to the back trail and spotted dust. Some moments later a stage-coach came into view. It was none of his business, he told himself. Still, if he rode quickly he could get down there by the time the coach arrived at where the men waited. Once he had been a lawman for a short time and the old instincts took hold of him. He put the glasses away into a saddlebag and headed Single on a diagonal course through the scrub guiding him expertly. A broken-legged horse would be of no use to him Thorne knew, and he'd hate like hell to have to put a bullet into Single. They were partners. He hadn't loved Sabrina Fairchild as much as he loved Single.

He could hear the coach coming, hear the hoofbeats, hear the wheels bumping over stone and hard ruts. He figured there'd be a shotgun guard. There might be women in the coach. He would have to be careful that they didn't mistake him for one of the bandits. He had seen them get mounted some minutes ago. He was some way behind them down the trail when he dismounted and climbed up on top of a boulder with his rifle. To shoot to kill one of those men would be murder, before he had seen what they intended. On the other hand he did not wish to see the stagedriver or the shotgun guard killed. A warning shot then.

The stage was within fifty yards

when one of the Mexicans came out on to the trail with his carbine levelled. The teamster hauled on the reins and slammed his foot on the brake handle. Thorne squeezed the trigger and the Mexican fell sideways from his horse which dashed off into the scrub just as the other two bandits came to the rear of the coach. They did not see their *compadre* leave the saddle, and probably assumed it was he who had fired the shot. They moved forward just as the shotgun guard swung round and blasted off a shot which threw up dirt in front of the left-hand rider. Cursing, he pulled away off the trail. The other one was almost at the stage-coach window when Thorne, who was now peering round from behind a prickly pear called to the bandit. "Drop your gun Pedro, or I'll blast you to hell."

The teamster who now had his rifle in his hands, heard Thorne and was somewhat mystified. He leaned over and saw the bandit look round, and then swing his horse away from the coach as a man stuck his head out.

Still being careful he wasn't being mistaken for a bandit, Thorne let off another shot as the bandit fled down the trail, hightailing it after his *compadre*.

Two men got out of the coach pistols in hands as Thorne stepped cautiously out on to the trail. "Hello there," he called. "Are you all right?"

Chuck Bowers looked at the teamster who'd now jumped down, but was keeping an eye on Thorne who had his rifle pointed down. "Was that you as killed that bandit up front?" he asked Thorne.

"Yes, I figured he was the most dangerous. I saw them from top of that hill. Thought they were after me, then I saw the coach coming."

"Wal, I'm mighty obliged, mister . . . " The teamster, Kyle Johnson, put out a hand.

Thorne took it. "Santiago," he said, as the others gathered round. He could see a smartly dressed Mexican woman put her head out from the coach. He had an idea he'd seen her before somewhere, but wasn't sure. He spoke with the driver and shotgun guard, telling them how he had happened to be where he was when the bandits tried to hold up the coach. He noted that the two men who spoke with the woman were American and wore side-guns and seemed very uneasy. Soon they were on their way again and Thorne, after mounting, rode on keeping an alert eye open.

When the dark came he went across the river and rode into El Paso, going down a back street. He went straight to the livery stable and handed Single over into the care of the ostler, leaving two dollars. Then taking his saddle-bags and rifle, he headed for a rooming-house he had used on other occasions. Sally Duvall welcomed Thorne with a big smile and a hug. "My lord, Santi, you stink like a dead buffalo," she said, and stood back holding her nose. "Where the devil you bin?"

Thorne didn't answer her question.

"Sal, I need a hot tub, a shave, and plenty of sleep. I'm whacked out," he told her.

She made a face at him. "I've got no free rooms, but you know where mine is. I'll get Ying to fetch hot water for you, it'll take a while to heat."

"Thanks Sal," said Thorne and went on through to the far end of a corridor and entered her private domain. It smelled of various perfumes and female. He put his bags and rifle under the bed. Sal was right, he did stink like a dead carcass, and he ached all over.

There were several bottles on a sideboard. He took a glass and poured himself a large bourbon, sat down on a reclining chair, and lit a cheroot. It would drive out the perfumy smell, he thought. He began to relax. Never again he told himself. The past weeks had been full of tension and sometimes real fear.

2

WHEN Thorne looked at his timepiece it was almost 9.30 a.m. He lay for a while enjoying the warmth and comfort. He sneezed violently as the perfume got to his nose. If he ever took a woman on a permanent basis, she'd have to get rid of such stuff. The best smells, in his opinion, were the good earthy ones of nature. Flowers in springtime, sage in bloom, pine trees and blossoms. Not the aromas of a cluttered-up room with bottles of imitation scents and all sorts of gewgaws.

Lifting himself on his elbows he still felt stiff in spite of the hot bath and scrubbing Ying had given him, after which he'd towelled himself vigorously. Sal had brought food for him but he had been too tired to eat more than a mouthful. He hadn't even noticed when she'd climbed in or when she'd left him, but he could see from her pillow she had slept there. Then, it was her bed; one he had shared on previous occasions, and when he'd been in better shape.

Thorne lay for a while in reflective mood. He ought to get up, but he'd not lain thus for quite some time and it felt good. His thoughts still dwelt on aromas. His very first kitten, he remembered, had had a special smell, and he'd often let it crawl in under the covers. His grandpa had always smelled of tobacco, his grandma of cooking, and on Sundays when she went to church, a slight whiff of scent. His mother had smelled special too, he thought bitterly. He was about five years old when she'd married a young army lieutenant and gone out West someplace. He'd cried himself to sleep a lot in those days. His father he hardly remembered. He had died when he was three, though later he had found out his pa had got drunk and fallen into the Potomac River and drowned. He'd never known his paternal grandparents because they had never left Connecticut, and he assumed they were dead now.

Wilhelm and Lotte Hasler, his maternal grandparents, had brought Rudi up, taken care of him, after their daughter Renata had married Charles Hennessy. The lieutenant had thought it best not to take a small boy with them to some Godforsaken outpost in Indian country. His mother had written at first, but the letters often had taken weeks to arrive, some never reaching his grandma at all. Once she had written asking for Rudi to be brought out to Fort Worth, but Willi Hasler had said, emphatically, no, the boy should stay and get his education, and he wasn't about to go all that way with Rudi.

The Haslers had lived comfortably, Willi making a decent living as a gunsmith, and had also repaired and sold clocks.

Thorne stirred himself and got out

of bed. He didn't wish to dwell on maudlin thoughts. His grandpa had died, almost blind, six years ago, and his grandma a year later. They had left him all they had which had turned out to be a fair nest-egg. After selling the house, giving up his job at the bank where he had worked since leaving school, Rudi had stored several valuable items in the bank vault, and taken passage on a ship out of Baltimore and gone down to New Orleans. He had spent some time there, but had found it sticky and hot, and had not really liked the people, many of whom had spoken a strange kind of French, or, some of them, Spanish. He'd had a yearning to get away from city life and had taken himself off westwards, perhaps hoping to find his mother. He had written after his grandpa had died to the last place she had been known to be, but had not received an answer. It was the only time he had ever tried communicating with her. He had found some letters from her in his grandma's private box. She couldn't have thought much of him to go off and leave him like that at a time when he had needed her so.

He looked around for his clothes and couldn't find them. His stomach rumbled angrily, and he cursed. Sally pushed open the door and came in bearing a tray full of breakfast food. "About time you were up," she said. "I've never known you to lie abed so late, least not alone," she laughed.

Thorne grinned. "I needed that sleep badly. Where the hell are my clothes?"

"Santi, they're soaking in a tub out back. Frankly, that doeskin jacket will never come clean," she said, nipping her nose between her fingers. "Just where do you go to get so stinking filthy?"

"It's not difficult down in that hot country. You can dump the jacket. Send Ying to get my bedroll, I have some things in there." Thorne told her. He pulled the saddle-bags out from under the bed and yanked out some underwear and a plaid shirt. He dropped the nightshirt Sal had loaned him as she sat down, quite unabashedly admiring his maleness. Well, she was seeing nothing she hadn't seen before.

Thorne still wasn't feeling particularly in the mood for a tumble with Sal. There had been a very desirable Spanish woman staying at Peter Varig's hacienda, and had he not been so preoccupied with other matters he'd have tried his luck there. Adelaide Mendosa had certainly eyed him with intimate interest across the dinner-table when Varig had put on a fine dinner for his guests that last evening. A sudden movement in his nether region made Thorne turn around quickly, he did not wish Sally Duvall to think it was she who'd inspired it. He was not unaware that she had a yen for him. She was only one of many.

Ying came in with the bedroll and Thorne fished out some cord pants and a black leather jacket. After he was dressed he sat down and ate the food. The last thing he did before leaving the room was to put on his holster belt, after checking the Colt. El Paso was a town to walk careful in, he thought.

Sally was in the kitchen drinking coffee. "You sure look a different *hombre*," she said admiringly, though Thorne detected a slight chill in her manner.

"Sleep, food and a hot bath can do wonders," he said. Feeling somewhat guilty he went out of the back door. "I'll see you later," he called over his shoulder. Why the hell should he feel guilty?

Going down a back street he thought about Sally. She was but a good friend; he owed her nothing. He liked her, that was all. He had not been ungenerous. He headed for the livery stable and Single gave a welcoming nicker and shoved Thorne in the ribs. The horse had been curried, he could see. He made a mental note to come back later and give the night ostler an extra dollar.

Next he went to the bank to see the manager.

"Ah, Mr Santiago!" Dick Emerson greeted him as he was ushered into his office.

Thorne took off his hat and pulled out the cheque from the inner band, and a handwritten note which he handed to Emerson. Emerson pulled a file from his desk drawer and did some checking.

Thorne looked anxious for a moment as the manager said a few 'Ah-ha's' to himself. "Yes, it is all right; though if I were you, I'd not take any more cheques from Mr Varig before you contact me."

Thorne relaxed. "I think my business with Varig is now completed. Can you let me have five hundred dollars, and transfer the commission to my account in Washington, as usual?" he asked Emerson.

"Of course, with pleasure," Emerson said, putting the cheque into the file after making a note.

Thorne left the bank after placing four $100 notes into his hat, and ten $10 into his wallet, then headed for the Saguaro Saloon. He had hardly taken two steps towards the bar when a voice hailed him. "Hey, Santi, *cómo está?*"

Thorne swore under his breath. He wasn't over anxious to see Pat Crenna. He was somewhat garrulous when he was on a drinking bout, which was most of the time when he was in funds. There was no avoiding him now.

Ordering a beer, Thorne took it across to the table where Crenna sat with a man dressed in range clothes and chaps. He pulled out a chair and sat down.

"Santi, what you been up to? You been a naughty boy? I hear a big shipment of repeater rifles was taken off a train bound for the Federales in Chihuahua," Crenna said, his voice carrying to the tables where at least one head turned to regard Thorne with some curiosity.

"I wouldn't know about that," Thorne

responded sharply, his eyes going cold, and suddenly Crenna lifted up his glass and took a long drink, emptying it. "Oh, this is Don Wells, a buddy of mine, he works at a ranch north of here."

Thorne nodded, then turned and called the bartender and put up three fingers. For a while he sat listening to Crenna's discourse on his latest attempt to find work. After finishing his second beer, Thorne got up. "I must go, Pat. See you around," he said and walked on out into the street thinking about the stolen guns.

Crenna watched him go, a dark look on his face. He'd learned nothing from Santiago. He, like many in the region, knew Thorne only as Santiago. He had helped him once freighting some boxes into Mexico which had been full of Smith and Wesson revolvers. It had been quite frightening at times. Twice they'd almost been caught by Federales, and then there'd been the Indians and bandits. Santiago was a devious fella, real cool though. He sure wished he knew if he had a deal going. He was down to his last five bucks and nothing on offer except range work which he had no liking for. Don worked his ass off chasing steers out of the *brasados* for little more than beer money. It wasn't for him. He called for a bottle of cheap Mexican brandy.

Don Wells got up. "I gotta go, Pat. You come to the ranch if you want that job, only don't wait long 'cos there's plenty needing work, and the Mexicans work cheap."

"Yeah, OK, Don. I'll think on it," Crenna replied. In a pig's eye would he. He could make more rolling a drunk in a back street. Damn it, he'd go watch for Santiago. He must have something going. He took the bottle and went to the livery where his horse was stabled. He gave the ostler two bits and went up the ladder into the hay loft and made himself comfortable above Thorne's horse. He knew it well.

Thorne had already made up his mind to move on and not spend another night in El Paso. He made his way to a hotel and sat in the foyer awhile reading the latest news which was a week old, he noticed. Then he went into the dining-room and ordered steak and what went with it. This was his favourite food. He finished up with apple pie and coffee. He sat thinking about the future. He ought to set down some roots, buy a piece of land. His thoughts turned to his last trip to Mexico. Others could have taken the guns, but he was the one trusted to bring back the payment after making sure they arrived there safely intact. Varig never parted with money until he saw the goods and he always paid by cheque.

Thorne was not a political man but he didn't like the present regime in Mexico. He'd learned a lot during his trips down there. Hate everywhere and cruelty on both sides. This time he had seen something he'd not been supposed to at Varig's place; a man tied to a pole upside down, and lashed raw. After he had screamed and told them what they wanted to know they had shot him. If he could have taken back the guns he would have done so. It suddenly came to him that Varig was playing his own game. Perhaps he stole back the rifles after selling them to whoever would pay the price he asked. Well, it was finished with. Thorne got up and went back to Sally's and spent over an hour playing mah-jong with Ying who had taught him the game a couple of years ago when he'd laid over a while.

Ying slammed one of the ivory-faced pieces down, grinning. "Velly sorry, Mr Santiago, you lose," he said.

Thorne laughed and placed two dollars on the table.

"Ying, if I get settled some place, would you come and be my housekeeper? Maybe I could get to beat you?"

The Chinaman gave Thorne a shrewd look. "You find good woman before too late. Me come when you ready, you send coach ticket. You promise no kick up ass like missee," he said, grinning.

"No Ying, I'd never do that," Thorne said thoughtfully.

Sally Duvall looked unhappily at Thorne when he told her he would not be staying. He handed her five dollars. "For the bed and grub," he said. "I can't stay in El Paso; there's a man in town I'd rather — well it's best I go. I probably won't be back this way, so take care, Sal. Maybe it would be best if you were to move east again — it's rough out here. Find yourself a good man to take care of you," he advised.

Sally laughed harshly. "Was a good man who brought me out here and left me," she said bitterly. "Perhaps when I've made a bit more dough. So long, Santi — don't take any wooden nickels," she said sadly.

Thorne stepped into the saddle. The night was cool and the stars bright. A waxing moon showed him the trail as he rode out of town around nine o'clock. He had slept a couple of hours, eaten again and he had a bottle of good bourbon in his saddle-bag. Before the light came he would be at the way-station. He had given some thought to selling Single, but he couldn't part with him, his good old friend who'd saved his life on one or two occasions. He would take his time and ride north to the spur line that would take him to the east-bound rail track. Once he had ridden through Wichita Falls; that's where he would head for, it had seemed a real nice place and the people friendly. After eight years of roaming lonesome, he was ready to settle. He had a considerable bank balance now. He whistled for a while as Single stepped out eager to go.

3

PAT CRENNA landed on the ground with a thump. He had fallen asleep and the horse had wandered off the track and stumbled over a mound. "Jeezus! Where the hell am I? You stupid lunkhead!" he cursed at the horse. With difficulty he got mounted again looking around and seeing the moon was over to his right now. He got the dun back to the trail. Where was Santi now he wondered? Might be bedded down somewhere. If he kept going and got ahead of him he would see him as the light came. "Dammit, Patrick you shouldn't have drunk all that brandy," Crenna muttered to himself. He thought about Santiago as he rode on clinging to the horn. Who was he? He'd always said that was the only name he had, like he'd been born poor like the Mexican peons. Yet, he'd heard him speaking German to Varig, and he had a good grasp of the Mex lingo. He must be carrying dough or on his way to pick some up, and I reckon he can spare plenty, it'll be a pleasure to take it off him. What if there's a reward on Santi? Yeah, might be I can make some enquiries, Crenna thought as the horse plodded onwards.

An hour after sun-up Crenna was riding towards a way-station. A southbound stage-coach stood outside and a few passengers were waiting to board. Amongst several horses tied at a hitching-rack, he could see Santiago's horse. It would look suspicious if he went in there, he would have to wait now until Santi came out, and he sure as hell needed breakfast. Just where could he be heading? Might be Santi knew somebody up this way who had the hardware. He got down and tied the reins round the horn and let the horse browse while he waited.

After eating breakfast, and making

a few enquiries of the stage driver, Thorne mounted the red and went on up the trail. He'd rested a couple of hours and he would rest again when it became hot. By ten o'clock by his timepiece, Thorne could feel the heat striking up at him from the parched ground. All around him was a shimmering hazy atmosphere. Nothing much stirred. He spoke to the horse. "Single, it's rest time," he said and went off the trail into a hollow by some cottonwood trees. He could have gone a quicker way to the railroad but that would have meant crossing over a hundred miles of gypsum dunes and scrub. If a horse went lame on a fella out there, he'd had it. He was in no real hurry, he was beginning to feel thoroughly relaxed.

He took the saddle off Single, tied up the reins and let him browse or stand as he pleased. After inspecting the ground for snakes he placed his bedroll and sank on to it, pulling his Colt round across his leg, and his hat over his face. He had taken a good look at his back-trail and seen no sign of anyone.

Crenna grinned when he saw the scuff marks where a horse had left the trail. He got down and led the dun carefully. When he spotted the form under the trees he smiled briefly. Santi was no fool, but he was surely a mite careless. Leaving the dun tied at a scrub bush, Crenna went forward stepping quietly. His luck had been down lately, all he had left was five bucks and no prospects. Santiago must have thousands, he figured. He drew his side-gun and moved on.

Single nickered and Thorne came alert. He did not move but his hand tightened on the Colt butt. It might be an animal. He hoped it wasn't Indians.

"All right, Santi! Just stay still or I'll have to plug yer," Crenna's voice came from Thorne's left.

"I'm not moving, Pat. What is it you want?"

"Dough, of course; I reckon you got plenty, an' you paid me chicken feed for that job I helped you with. Might be the army would be interested to know about that," Crenna said, and moved closer.

Thorne moved his head slightly and his hat fell off his face. Now he could see Crenna standing about five yards away pointing his pistol at him. He moved again and sat up. Crenna was no cold-blooded murderer, he gambled.

"Just throw out all the dough you got in your poke, Santi — well, you can keep five bucks. I guess you can telegraph for more when you get to a telegraph office, and a bank."

"OK, hold your water," Thorne said and reached for his wallet, carefully. He extracted fifty dollars. "That's all there is," he lied. "I never carry much on account of trailbums like you." Thorne placed the folded ten-dollar notes on a tree root a couple of feet away.

Crenna ran his tongue around his lips looking anxiously at the bills. He'd expected more. Perhaps he should take the horse too. He moved forward gingerly, his eyes on Thorne. When he got to the root he hesitated. Then slowly he bent his knees, still watching Thorne and reached with his left hand for the bills.

Thorne was watching him carefully. Just before Crenna got his hand on the bills he looked down, as Thorne had calculated. Thorne, in one swift move, swept the gun hand aside and lashed out with a foot at Crenna catching him in the mouth.

Crenna shrieked, the pistol went off into the ground and Thorne grabbed him by the front of his jacket and swung him round up against the tree bole. He took the gun from Crenna's hand. Blood was pouring from his mouth and a couple of teeth were gone.

"You piece of low life, Crenna. If you had asked nicely in El Paso, I'd've given you a few bucks. I owe you nothing. You accepted that job and

I paid you three hundred dollars, fed you and supplied you with a horse."

Crenna was whimpering and holding a dirty handkerchief to his mouth. "You bastard! How can I eat with no teeth, and the females ain't going to look at me now? I got no dough and no job — *nada*!" he said.

Thorne picked up the money and stuffed it into Crenna's shirt pocket. "Here, take it! You never should have tried it, you're too slow. A real bum would've shot me and then taken the dough. I guess I'd better be more careful in future," he said.

Thorne shucked the bullets from Crenna's pistol, then he saddled up Single and rode up out of the hollow. At the rim he turned and called back. "You'd better not follow me, Crenna. Next time I might have to kill you!" Then he was gone back to the trail and loping northwards.

Crenna sat against the tree wallowing in self-pity. Even the fifty bucks didn't console him. All he could think about was what the females would think of him with his two front teeth missing. "Oh, Jesus!" he wailed.

The following afternoon Thorne rode into Las Cruces. A feeling of melancholy had suddenly come over him. He was a lonesome man, but he'd never felt the need for mates as some men did. Even when he had worked in the bank after leaving school, he hadn't joined in with his colleagues much. He had never drunk to excess, though he enjoyed liquor when he wanted it. He smoked little cheroots, as his grandpa had done. He had never done anything to extreme. Tonight he would seek company — it had been a long time since he'd indulged himself. He would lay over a day or two and give the horse a rest. He would not ride Single down, he had done a lot of miles these past weeks.

The hotel for this part of the country was as good as one could expect, Thorne knew. He stashed his rifle and saddle-bags in the wardrobe, then took off his jacket, boots and hat and lay stretched on the bed.

It was almost 8 p.m. when he awoke and quite dark. Ten minutes later he was tucking into a large steak and vegetables, and enjoying a glass of beer. Suddenly there was a silence in the dining-room and Thorne heard the two men sitting next to him suck in their breath. He turned his head and saw the Mexican woman, dressed in a black dress with full skirt and long sleeves, with a multi-coloured shawl draped around her shoulders, sweep in escorted by two Anglos dressed in dark suits. It was the woman whom he had seen in the coach in Mexico and the men were the same two, he now saw. There wasn't a lot of choice on the menu, but he'd noticed *enchiladas de pollo*. She might like that.

Thorne was reading a month-old newspaper in the lounge when he felt a presence and looked up. It was the woman and she reeked of perfume. He stifled a sneeze as he got up hurriedly.

"*Señor*, it is you. I thought so," she said, smiling. "You remember, the bandits . . . "

"Yes, I remember," Thorne said. "Who could ever forget such a beautiful woman as you, *señora*."

Estelle Singer smiled graciously, she was not averse to a genuine compliment. "I never got to thank you properly," she said. "It might have been quite different if you had not come along."

"Indeed it might," said Thorne. "Sometimes things happen like that."

"May one ask your name?" Estelle said softly.

"Santiago," said Thorne telling the lie for the umpteenth time, and wondering about the woman who travelled with the two American escorts.

"I'm Estelle Singer, and my husband has a hacienda west of Hatch. Santiago! *Señor*, then you're Spanish."

"No, *señora*, American," Thorne replied and saw a lift to the corners of her lips.

"My husband also," she replied.

One of the men standing a few feet away, coughed.

"I'm afraid I must go, *señor*. I must send a telegraph to my husband to say we are somewhat delayed. I wish you a pleasant evening," Estelle told Thorne and swept on up the staircase, her two bloodhounds following behind her.

Thorne was thinking it was unusual for a Mexican woman such as Estelle Singer to be travelling without her maid. He hadn't liked the look of her two escorts; he was sure they had been wearing shoulder holsters under their jackets. Well, she was married to an American and had probably changed her lifestyle. He finished a brandy and went out into the street. After walking for some minutes he turned into a side street and came to a largish clapboard house he had visited previously.

A woman of ample proportions greeted him in the garish, plushy-red foyer. "Is Geena still here?" Thorne asked her without more to-do.

"Geena, ah no! I'm afraid she moved

on. Let me see, there is Bridget, the redhead over there. She should suit you," Moll Parker said, businesslike. "It'll be twenty-five dollars. She's one of my top girls."

Thorne produced the money. "Send her up — I hope she's worth it," he said coldly. How he hated this performance, paying for a woman. It was purely animalistic. He'd rather have been with Estelle Singer; there had been a mutual attraction there, he felt sure of it.

Moll Parker was not well pleased when Thorne did not come down until well past midnight. She remonstrated with him. "I had another customer waiting, and he is a regular."

"For twenty-five bucks, I could get ten Mex girls as good as Bridget," Thorne told her sharply.

Moll closed the door after him with a slam and gave out with a nasty expletive.

When Thorne got back to the hotel he saw there was no one at the desk so he went round and pulled out the registration book and took a look at it. Mrs Singer was in number 16, a J. Durrant in 12, and F. Danson in 13, and all were from the Vista Hermosa Hacienda, Hatch.

Thorne's registration simply said, Snr Santiago, and an address in Washington, which if anyone were to enquire there for him, would meet a dead end.

He went on up to his room, thinking about Estelle Singer and it came to him that he had seen her when he had stopped at a village just out of the Madero valley where Varig had his hideout. She was talking to a tall Mexican in animated fashion. He wondered what she had been doing down there. He got undressed and slid under the sheets. It had been a long day.

4

WHEN Thorne went down for his breakfast, Estelle Singer and the two men were just leaving. She looked as if she'd had a restless night. "Good morning, *señora*," he said. "I trust you slept well." His eyes held hers and she answered him rather self-consciously.

"Quite well thank you!"

"Are you expecting to get on your journey today?" Thorne enquired, noting the uneasiness of the two men.

"We're not sure, there seems to be no room on the coach and they haven't a spare one as yet."

"That's unfortunate," said Thorne.

She shrugged. "As they say, these things happen!" She turned to the younger man. "Jack, we'd better send another telegraph," and swept on up the stairs.

After he'd breakfasted Thorne went to see Single who seemed quite contented. He spoke with the ostler, a middle-aged, grey-haired man with a pronounced limp. "Do you know of a man called Singer? I believe he has a hacienda near Hatch."

"Sure, everybody knows Max Singer — leastwise the local folks do."

Thorne smiled. Hatch was a good forty miles north, then that was local out here in this vast land. "His wife is staying at the hotel. She's some looker!"

"That she be! She sure got a fiery temper that one. Singer took on plenty when he married her. She's his second wife, so I heard. He's into his forties. I reckon she married him for his dough. He got plenty. He's real jealous if any fella gets too close to her. I heard he almost put a bullet into one of them Mex dons who was visiting. Seen him knocking on her boudoir door. They got a room each. Them rich folks got queer ideas. They got too many bedrooms, I reckon!"

Thorne laughed. "Perhaps he snores," he said.

When he got back to the hotel he was surprised to see Estelle in the lounge drinking coffee with her two escorts. He went in and ordered some, taking an old newspaper off a stand with him. Time now meant nothing to him. He was feeling more relaxed than he had in months. He always enjoyed observing people, and meeting them in the different places he landed in.

The boy brought him a pot of coffee. He was on his second cup when a crash made him turn his head, so did others. The man he now knew to be Jack Durrant lay on the floor holding his belly and moaning. Estelle Singer was leaning over him. "Get a doctor, someone," she called out to the waiter.

The lad ran to the foyer where he found the manager at the desk. He sent him to get the doctor and came striding through to the lounge.

Thorne got up and went over. Durrant had stopped squirming and the manager and Danson, his fellow traveller, got him on to the couch. A few minutes later a doctor came in and quickly opened his bag. After taking his pulse, sounding his chest, looking into his eyes and mouth, he said. "He might have had a fit. Let's get him up to his room. Everyone stand back."

"We've checked out," Estelle said, looking pale. "Now we won't be able to travel." She looked at the manager, pleadingly.

"The rooms have not been taken yet, madam, you may have them," he assured her.

Thorne sat down again. Damned odd he thought. Durrant looked as if he'd been drugged. He'd seen a similar case in Mexico. Down there the people used all kinds of things they picked off trees or shrubs. Many of the seeds were poisonous. The peasant folks in particular knew all about them. About midday he decided to go for a beer and ate a ham sandwich, then went up for a nap until the heat had subsided. When he arrived at his door, Estelle Singer was just entering her room. "How is Durrant?" he called to her.

"He'll be all right, I think. The doctor thinks he has had some bad food. He's given him a potion. In any case, we can't leave today." She was about to go in then turned. "Santiago, do you have any whiskey?"

Somewhat surprised, Thorne said, "Yes, well, it's bourbon. I'll go get some whiskey if you wish."

"Bourbon will do," she replied. "Please, may I drink it in your room. I don't want the smell of it in mine. I — er . . . "

"Of course," Thorne said, again surprised.

She came along and after looking along the corridor followed Thorne inside and closed the door.

"Shouldn't you leave that open?" Thorne asked her.

She looked at him, her eyes mocking,

a smile on her lips. "You afraid of your reputation, Señor Santiago?" she said.

"Not mine, yours. What if your husband should suddenly turn up? I hear he's got something of a temper," Thorne said evenly.

Estelle's eyes hardened, he saw a spark of annoyance in them. "So you've been prying?" she said and took a long swig of her bourbon. "That's powerful stuff! To be honest I prefer a good tequila or brandy."

Thorne smiled. He found his heartbeat suddenly speeding up. "You're quite Americanized, I see."

"That's right, but I still care for my country. Do you have one you care for? Or, is it just a sport to you — gun-running? A way to make a fast buck?"

It was Thorne's turn to show anger. "You too seem to have been prying, *señora*," he said coldly. Possibly Durrant had heard of him. He had heard of him somewhere, but right now he couldn't think where.

"It came to me this morning where I heard about you. Santiago, the elusive one. Adelaide Mendosa is a friend of mine. She thinks you are one terrific *hombre*," Estelle said and finished her drink.

Thorne took her empty glass and poured out another shot of bourbon. "That is pure speculation on her part. The only time we laid eyes on each other was across a table when a friend of mine gave a dinner party for some of his friends," he told her, somewhat heatedly.

"Peter Varig! That one! Do you think your guns will help? Do you care who they will kill?" Estelle's eyes blazed.

Thorne was seated on the bed and she on a chair. "There'll be no more guns from me. This present regime is a dictatorship, and someone has to help stop them. But I saw enough down there this time to convince me that each side, or group, is as treacherous and cruel as the other. I'm finished with it!" Thorne said angrily.

"You know nothing," Estelle said vehemently. "My father and brother are both dead. Shot by soldiers who did as they were told, and they enjoyed it. My mother and sister are in hiding. I took a risk going down there but when I got there they had gone. I did not see them. My husband got me out of it after my father was killed."

"Like I said, it's none of my business. I'm through with it," Thorne reiterated, lamely.

"Where are you going now, if I may ask?" said Estelle, putting down her glass.

"No place in particular. Wherever I feel like going. Just me and Single," Thorne told her.

"Single, who is Single?" she enquired, her eyes now bland again.

"My horse!" Thorne grinned and his face lit up.

"A horse! Why Single?" she asked laughing.

"Well, there were two horses for sale

by the vendor and I couldn't make up my mind. He said you want both or just the single. Just then the one next to me gave a shove, so I said, 'Single, just the single'. I have to ride everywhere now if there's no rail track, as I couldn't possibly part with that horse."

Estelle got up from her chair. She looked at Thorne, a gleam in her eyes. "I bet your name isn't Santiago," she said as she put down her glass. "You're quite a mystery, mister whoever-you-are. I can see why Adelaide was so impressed. Thanks for the bourbon; I feel much better now," she said, and opened the door and was gone before Thorne could reply.

Thorne got up off the bed and stretched. If she'd stayed a minute longer he would have grabbed her. Damn the woman, she was playing with him.

There was no sign of Estelle in the dining-room, only Fred Danson. Thorne went to ask after Durrant.

"He's sleeping. The Doc's been again and says he'll probably be all right by tomorrow, so we can go."

"He doesn't take any kind of drug, does he?" Thorne asked Danson, watching him closely.

Danson seemed shaken for a moment. "Jack, no! He would never do that, and he don't drink a lot. Mr Singer would kick him out if he did."

"You both work for Singer then?"

"Sure, have done for two years. He pays well," said Danson.

"Well, I'm glad Durrant is all right," said Thorne, though it was of little consequence to him; he didn't like the man, and he couldn't say why, he hardly knew him. He went on over to the saloon and got into a game of poker. He won some and lost some; he hadn't played for some time. Just before he left the saloon he saw Crenna at a table in a corner. He hoped the fool wasn't still following him.

It seemed he had hardly got to sleep when a soft tap at his door woke Thorne up. He lit the lamp and looked at his timepiece. By God, it was almost 1.30. "Who is it?" he asked near the door.

"Santiago, are you awake?" A feminine voice spoke in a whisper close to the door.

Puzzled, Thorne opened it a fraction. To his surprise he found Estelle Singer standing there, with a bottle of whiskey in her hands, and clad in her dressing-gown. "I can't sleep," she said. "I'm scared."

Thorne pulled her in quickly, took a quick look down the corridor and then closed the door. "Scared, why?" he asked, feeling uneasy.

"Some men have come into town. Fred Danson saw them. They have been after us. We thought we had shaken them off some days ago, before we bumped into you."

"Why are they after you? Who are they?" Thorne asked. Then he said, "Why didn't Danson go to the sheriff?"

"We don't want the sheriff. They are

probably some Federales; agents. They might be looking for me. Someone must have seen me and told them. They are sure to have Yankee papers, so the sheriff, he could do nothing. Please, Señor Santiago, help me get to Hatch. My husband will be there with men. I'll pay you. Only two days, please," she pleaded.

"Listen, my dear, I'm finished with all that. It is not my war. Your husband should have been with you."

"He can't ever go back to Mexico. He killed an important government man," she said angrily. "Here, I got some whiskey." She handed him the bottle.

Thorne's instinct told him to send her back to her room, and then go get Single and ride on out. Something was wrong. He should get away from her. Yet, she did seem quite genuinely afraid. It was odd though, that Durrant was the only one ill if it had been food poisoning. They must have all eaten the same things.

"I'm not a drinker," he said and put the bottle on the washstand. "Why don't you go and get some sleep?" he told her.

"I'm afraid! I told you! Danson is with Durrant and I don't want to go in there. Durrant — he well, he is much too familiar at times."

Thorne thought for a moment as he stood in his nightshirt, feeling foolish. Then he locked the door. "All right. You take the bed and I'll use the chair. You look all in," he said kindly. Had he misjudged her? He took the bed cover and wrapped it around himself and settled into the chair. As Estelle got under the covers he caught a brief sight of a bare leg. Christ! Didn't she have anything on under that gown? She was behaving like a tart, he thought. He turned the lamp down.

Thorne couldn't sleep. The chair wasn't large enough and he could smell female. He got up and lit a cheroot.

"*Mi querido*, can't you sleep?" she called to him. "The chair, it can't be

59

comfortable. Come, there is plenty of room here. I won't bite you," she laughed throatily.

Thorne stubbed out the cheroot. Damn it, he was not made of ice! She was a full grown woman, probably his age, or a bit older. If that was what she wanted then he would oblige her. He dropped his nightshirt and slid in beside her.

"Santiago, you will help me tomorrow, won't you?" she whispered close to his ear.

"I'll think about it," he said and pulled her in to him. He felt the smile on her lips as her hand slid over his belly.

5

A WAGON rattling down the street awoke Thorne and he sat up suddenly. His bed smelled of female, but she was gone. It was just sun-up as he lay back thinking about Estelle Singer. She was some woman, by God! He stretched like a cat. Why had she offered herself in such abandonment? He would have helped her anyway. What man could resist those pleading black eyes? He got dressed and went down to the dining-room. He wondered if Crenna was still in town. After finishing his breakfast he went on down to the livery barn. The man with the game leg was there. "Is there anyone up top?" he asked. "A man in his twenties, dark hair?"

"Oh, him! Yeah he's up there. Though what state he'll be in, I couldn't say. Be my guest," Webster told Thorne and went to the tack room.

Thorne went up the ladder and found Crenna curled up in a corner on a pile of hay. He shook him. "Crenna, wake up. I want to talk to you."

"What? Who is it? Whadya want?" Crenna's eyes came open. He saw Thorne and, cringing, let out a shriek, putting up his arms to fend Thorne off. "Leave me alone, you bastard." His breath stank of liquor and Thorne backed up.

"I won't hurt you. I just want to talk with you. Come on down and we'll go have some breakfast." Christ! he really had scared Crenna. Suddenly Thorne felt sorry for him.

Crenna came down the ladder very carefully, his eyes bloodshot, and with the two teeth missing he looked a sorry sight. He was not a large man, but he was lean, strong, and had handled himself well when Thorne had hired him two years ago to go into

Mexico. He could ride and handle horses with expertise. After he had sluiced himself down at a water trough, they went over to a café the teamsters and rangemen used.

"What you want, Santi?" Crenna asked after he'd drunk a mug of coffee.

"I might have a job for you. Not certain but almost. A couple of days."

"I don't know as I wanna work with you again. You play dirty. Now I can't get a woman, the way I look."

"Damn it, Crenna. You held a gun on me. You were about to rob me, perhaps kill me. Besides I didn't intend knocking your teeth out. And why are you on my trail?"

"I ain't following you. It's better here than in El Paso. Might be I can get some work here."

"Listen, there's a woman who wants me to help escort her to Hatch."

Crenna's eyes showed a spark of interest. A female. "What? Which one? Why you need me?"

"She's Mexican. I met her on the

trail to El Paso when three bandits tried to hold up the stage. She's here in the hotel with two men. One of them got sick. They may be leaving today. She's worried because she believes there's two other men after her from Mexico. I've not seen them, but we could watch out for them on the trail."

"Why they after her?" Crenna asked, suspicious.

"I'm not sure. Might be agents out of Mexico — you know how it is there, all politics. She might be carrying something. It's not my concern. If you're not interested, I understand," Thorne said and got up.

"What are you paying?" Crenna asked casually.

"Half of what she pays me. I don't know how much yet. I'm riding that way, so why not help her?"

"Sounds odd to me. I don't like the sound of the two Mexicans. Why can't her two escorts see to them?"

"They'll be in the coach. We're just extra protection, that's all."

Crenna grinned. "I guess you got yourself some female trouble, Santi. OK I'm in. When do we go?"

"I'm not sure, you stay here. I'll be back. No more booze — *comprende*?" Thorne said smiling.

"*Si, mi comprende*, Señor Santiago," said Crenna. Yeah I sure *comprende* all right. Now he needs me.

When Thorne got back to the hotel he found Danson and Durrant in the foyer. "You recovered?" he asked Durrant, who gave him a sharp look.

"I guess I'll live," he said gruffly.

"Will you be leaving on the stage at ten?" Thorne asked, feeling rather uneasy.

Durrant looked hesitant. "It's likely," he said.

Just then Estelle came down the stairs carrying her travel bag, Thorne noted, wondering why one of the men had not carried it for her. She greeted him casually, not meeting his eyes. "Good morning, Señor Santiago."

"Good morning, Señora Singer. You

hoping to get on your way, I see."

"I think so. Fred," — she turned to Danson — "will you check, see what time we can leave?" she asked him.

Danson, looking flustered, went out the door in a hurry. Estelle turned towards the dining-room with Durrant behind her. Thorne felt he'd been snubbed. Was she just going to ignore him? Had last night meant nothing to her? Had she changed her mind about his helping her? He went on up to his room to pack.

When he opened the door he saw an envelope on the floor. He picked it up and tore it open. It reeked of perfume and he sneezed. Inside was a sheet of paper and a $100 note. It read: 'Santiago *querido*, follow the coach, do not let those men get me. Stay out of sight. I have my little gun. We leave from behind the livery at 9.45 in a special coach. You are *muy mucho hombre. Hasta la vista.*'

Thorne folded the note and placed it in his inner pocket, the bill into his wallet. A strange expression crossed his face. By God, he'd never been paid for love before and that, he believed, was what it was all about. He had seen no strange men in town.

The black stage-coach with a yellow stripe along its side, drawn by four horses, took off with a flourish, as Crenna watched from his place by the hay-loft window.

Thorne in amongst some trees couldn't see who sat inside, but he saw the teamster clicking up the horses, with Fred Danson at his side, in the role of shotgun guard. Durrant must be inside with Estelle, then, he thought. What the hell was it all about? Why did men from Mexico seek her? If indeed they did. What had she been up to down there? If her father and brother had been shot, they must have been involved in politics. She obviously felt strongly about things down there. He let the coach get well up the trail before he followed.

Thorne rode between the trail and the

river. It was harder going but afforded better cover. If there were two men following, they might well be across the river. They might be anywhere. He hoped Pat Crenna was keeping an eye out. He'd almost regretted getting him involved now, but he felt sorry for him. The ostler had said there was a way-station about halfway to Hatch. It was a rough trail so the coach could not make fast progress. If all went well, they should be there by late afternoon. They would get fresh horses but he would not, so Single had a hard day's work ahead. It certainly was not a two-day job, he thought. Could be an easy fifty bucks each for him and Crenna.

It was about two hours after leaving Las Cruces that Thorne heard a low whistle and turned in his saddle. A few minutes later Crenna came up to him grinning.

"If you found me so easy, then so might others. Have you seen anyone?" Thorne asked him.

"I seen only two rangemen across the

river going west, and a wagon going south. I reckon nobody has seen you. The coach isn't far off the way-station now. I figured if I was to go in, they'd not know me. Might be I can learn something. You want I get you a sandwich?" said Crenna.

"Yes, good. That's the best thing to do," said Thorne. He was suddenly glad of Crenna's company. "You seem in better spirits. I've been thinking. You could get your teeth fixed by a special dentist. He could fix two in the slot for you."

"Oh yeah! And how much is that going to cost?" said Crenna, sarcastically.

"Probably a hundred bucks. It'd be worth it," Thorne said, sheepishly.

"I better get going. See you later," Crenna said and rode away to the river.

★ ★ ★

Estelle Singer was feeling hot and tired and edgy. She hoped all her planning would work, then she would be rid of Max, that pig, and Durrant too when she had finished with him. If only she had met Santiago much sooner. Too bad he might have to die, such an *hombre*. She thought of Don Diego de Silva. How strange that he should come back into her life again. He had brought news of her mother and sister to the village where she had gone to meet them. Thank God they were safe to Vera Cruz from where they would go to Venezuela to her uncle's plantation. If only she could have got rid of Danson and Durrant in Mexico. Diego had bungled it and Santiago had come along at the most inconvenient time. Well, at least she had found out about Max and how he had betrayed her father. She'd always felt he had. Now she knew. He must have the diamonds he and her father had brought up from South America, and probably more emeralds. He must have a lot of money stashed somewhere. But that pig Kugler never let her get near the bureau when Max was out. She was quite terrified of him. Even Jack was scared of him. She had some emeralds and a few diamonds inside the silver candlesticks Diego had given her. Safer with her he thought. Her mother had left them for her. She would be able to buy her way to Venezuela. Diego would meet her in Laredo, he would wait there for her. She must get Santiago to help her. Durrant she did not trust. First she must see what was in that bureau — it was hers. To hell with Max and his damned obsession with his horses. She was bored to hell with it. She crossed herself quickly.

★ ★ ★

Crenna rode into the way-station a little behind the coach. He took his horse to the water trough and watched from under his hat brim to see who got out. The driver and Danson got down. Danson went to the coach, opened the door and spoke with someone inside.

71

He went on over with the driver to the café while a man came to take the horses away and bring out fresh ones. So the lady was not getting out, Pat thought. He sauntered over and went inside and ordered a beer taking it to a side table. He noted three men at a long table, one wearing a star. He watched Danson pick up a beef sandwich and some lemonade which he took out to the coach. It sure must be hot in there with the blinds drawn down. Five minutes later the regular coach rolled in.

Thorne was puzzled. He had thought Estelle would not be staying long, but the second coach was loaded up and off within the half-hour, and still the black coach sat there. What if she had slipped on to the other coach? Well it did not matter really, he had been paid, and so long as she got safely to Hatch . . . He glanced skywards, it looked like rain and he had heard thunder rolling to the north. It was sticky but less hot than in El Paso. Thorne looked forward to a good night's sleep. Then he would move on at his leisure, perhaps take Pat Crenna with him. Get him to a decent town where he might find work.

It came to Thorne that he had not seen Durrant. Where the hell was he? The coach was moving now. What if it was just a decoy? Where was Pat? he wondered, suddenly feeling tired.

The coach was gone out of sight around a bend when Crenna came riding along the trail, loping steadily. A half-mile further along he swung off to his right. Thorne came out from behind a tree and whistled.

"Hey, Santi. *Comó está?*" Crenna greeted him. "You look worried, *amigo*!"

"What did you find out?" Thorne asked. "Was the woman there?"

"Yeah, she never got out, but I seen her just before they took off again — she went to the outhouse."

"Was Durrant in there too?"

"I reckon they would have taken him food if he had been, and he'd have gone to use the toilet."

"Then he must be riding a hired horse. Or it might be he wasn't fit to travel, after all," Thorne said, thinking it over. "Listen Pat, if anything should happen, you stay out of it. I don't want your death on my conscience. You understand?"

"*Si comprende*, Señor Santi. I let some sonofabitch shoot you. OK?" Crenna said. "Eez *mucho* pleasure, *señor*."

"All right, Pat, cut the sarcasm. If you should see someone drawing a bead on me, shoot the bastard. But if I get taken, stay clear: they'll kill you," Thorne told Crenna, who was now looking suitably impressed.

"You're sure taking it to heart, boss. That female must be something," Crenna said, tucking the fifty bucks Thorne passed to him down his boot. He jigged his horse away through the trees. Might be this Durrant fella was riding point, he thought. Pat Crenna had spent two years in the army as a horse soldier up in the Snake River country, before he deserted five years ago. He still often thought in army terms.

By late afternoon the black coach suddenly took a left turn off the trail into a fork road. Now that is interesting thought Crenna as he sat on a bluff using the spyglass that Thorne had bought for him after he had made certain they were on their way. He really felt more respect for Santi now who was really sorry about kicking his teeth in. Nobody had ever felt sorry for Pat, as he recalled. Not even his pa who had once beaten him badly with his belt. Nor had that bastard sergeant who'd spread him on a wagon wheel and flayed him raw, just because he had fancied his daughter. That was when he decided to quit the army before he killed that ignorant pig.

The coach was going across the river as Pat put the glass away. He hoped Santi had noticed. They were supposed to be going to Hatch and it wasn't that far now, so what were they playing at?

Suddenly he saw a flash of colour down in the trees and it wasn't Santiago's red, it was much darker. Where the hell are you, Santi?

Thorne looked anxiously around him. He had seen the coach leave the main trail, but he could not see Pat. He sweated. Why had they turned off, was it a short cut? But Estelle had said her husband would be in Hatch waiting for her. He heard a twig snap and drew in his breath sharply when he saw the dark horse angling towards the track, and he recognized the grey jacket Durrant had worn this morning. So, he had not been in the coach. There had been no sign of him until now. Estelle had said she was worried about him. What was he up to? Thorne followed cautiously.

★ ★ ★

Estelle had changed out of her dress into a leather skirt and shirt, short boots, and a cotton jacket. She sat with her travel bag beside her, hearing the thunder rolling some way off. She was worried. She had no idea why they had left the main trail, though it was possible to get on to the track going to the ranch. Had Durrant decided to do something now? But why? Where was he? The coach left the river and was now passing between stands of piñon and cottonwood.

A rifle cracked twice and Fred Danson threw up his arms and fell off the seat on to the trail. The young teamster, believing they were under attack from Indians or robbers, slapped the reins and yelled at the horses to get going. The coach lurched from side to side and Estelle was thrown violently against the framework and was knocked out.

Thorne took off, pulling out his rifle. He had seen Durrant lift his rifle and shoot at Danson, and could hardly believe his eyes. He could see him now racing after the coach. Suddenly a wheel struck a large stone and it went over. The coach was dragged for some yards until the horses, their legs tangled in the reins and tongue, pulled up. The young driver had been thrown clean over into the scrub.

Durrant got to the coach, lifted up the door and saw Estelle lying on the floor out cold. He reached in and took her travel bag, placing it over the horn and was about to ride off when he heard hoofs pounding and rifle fire. He felt a hot sensation go through his arm and drew up.

Max Singer, with three wranglers and his devoted guard, Kugler, came along the track just as Thorne had made the shot at Durrant. The big yellow-haired, square-faced man came at him and threw a loop over his shoulders, and he dropped the rifle. "Hey, what the hell are you doing? I'm not . . . "

"Shut your mouth you lousy bum," the big man told him.

"Oh hell, stay away Pat," Thorne muttered, now quite scared. The man had piggy eyes and powerful arms. He struggled to get loose as the man came alongside and grabbed the reins. The horse snorted so he hit it over the nose with his rifle.

"Hey, stop that. Get the rope off me, I'm not a bandit," Thorne yelled at him.

"Shut up, I told you," the man hit Thorne in the mouth and drew the rope tighter.

Right away Thorne guessed the older man dressed in britches and cord jacket, with long shiny boots, was Estelle Singer's husband. He too had a square face, dark eyes though and darker complexion. An Austrian, Thorne figured, especially when he heard the guttural accent.

Singer pushed Thorne's horse. "I'll deal with him later. Where's Jack?" he asked a thin-faced, tall wrangler.

After seeing the riders coming, Durrant made no further attempt to flee, especially after he felt the pain in his arm. Someone had hit him by accident, he figured. He was surprised when he saw Santiago tied up. Where the hell had he come from? "Hi boss," he said. "Glad you got here in time."

"Where's my wife?" Singer pushed past him.

"She's inside. I guess she got knocked out when the coach turned over. My arm, I can't . . . "

"Give me a hand somebody." Singer ignored Durrant.

A wrangler called Cooper got up and managed to haul Estelle out and hand her down, and placed her on the ground.

Thorne had seated himself on a rock and was watching anxiously. The yellow-haired man took out a stogey and lit it, still keeping an eye on him. Thorne was surprised when he saw Estelle had changed her clothes. What the hell had been going on? Whatever it was had gone wrong, he decided. He suddenly thought of the young driver. "Hey," he looked at the big one. "The driver, he must be lying somewhere. Perhaps he needs help."

Durrant, who was tying a bandanna

around his arm, heard. He came forward, ignoring Thorne like he did not know him and went on down the track. A few minutes later there were two shots. Durrant came back. "He tried to shoot me," he said, and put his Colt back into its holster. No one said a word.

Singer had put his jacket under Estelle's head and was leaning over her, sheltering her from the rain spots which were now falling. "Get the coach up," he called to Cooper. "Erich, you help him," he shouted.

"It was Danson," Durrant stood near Singer. "I guess that's why Mrs Singer had me riding out. There was no room in the regular coach so we had to hire this one," he told Singer.

"I figured something like that. You're three days late. I got the telegraph this morning," Singer said brusquely. He was puzzled, especially about Danson.

Estelle came round and moaned, her eyes opened. She spoke incoherently. "Papa, don't let them hurt me." She fought Singer off as he leaned over her.

"Stell, it's me, Max. You're OK. We'll get you home soon. Lie still," Singer told her.

The coach had been righted and, fortunately, only a spoke had been broken and there was scratching along its side. The horses were sorted out and hitched up again.

"Erich, you bring that sonofabitch along. I'll talk to him later."

"What about the two dead men?" Cooper enquired.

"You ride my horse, put one on yours, and one on Jack's, he can ride inside with me. You can bury them later at the hacienda," said Singer and got into the coach to sit opposite Estelle who'd been placed on the other seat.

"Get your horse, you," Kugler told Thorne, giving him a shove. "I sure wouldn't like to be in your shoes," he said, sniggering.

6

PAT had kept well back as Thorne had instructed him. He had watched it all through his spyglass as he sat up in a cottonwood, his horse tethered below. It didn't look good; he figured everything had gone wrong for Thorne. He had seen Durrant suddenly appear from nowhere and shoot Danson off the box and then seen Thorne shoot at Durrant. When he heard the hoofs pounding, he had got down to quiet his horse, and then moved on to get a closer view. He wished he understood what was going on. He couldn't just let Santi get killed, but there was little he could do against about half a dozen he could see pounding along the trail, and firing off shots. Moving amongst the scrub, he saw a big yellow-haired man throw a loop over Santi, and then hit him, as he tried to say something. Well, it looked as if Santi had had it now.

Leaving his dun tied, he crept forward to see what they were up to. He heard voices and saw a heavy-set man giving orders, the coach was put back up and the horses reined up again. When Durrant came back Crenna lay flat. He saw him pull his side-gun and put two shots into someone lying on the ground. Jeezus! he'd shot the coach driver while he was lying there. A while later the coach was rumbling along the trail the riders following, taking two dead bodies with them.

★ ★ ★

The coach was driven through an archway into a square inner yard. Thorne noted the Spanish-style hacienda. At one side a lot of horses were poking their heads out from loose boxes. Singer must be a man of wealth, he reckoned. Outside the inner fencing was grassland, though sun-scorched and dried up now through lack of rain. The thunder had died away.

"Get down," the big one told him, somewhat gutturally.

"Will you see to my horse?" Thorne asked anxiously. "I'd like my saddlebags, please."

Kugler laughed harshly. "Oh, and you'd like a hot bath drawn, too," he said, and pushed Thorne up against the adobe wall. Thorne winced and said, "*Schweinhund*", under his breath. Kugler tied his hands behind his back and then stood awaiting orders.

Estelle had been carried inside and a couple of Mexican women, wringing their hands, ran in after Singer who had yelled for them.

Most of the men had vanished quickly, except the big one, as Thorne thought of him. Kugler was smoking a stogey and then he called to an elderly peon to fetch him some water.

Eventually Singer and Durrant came out again. "You, what's your name?" Singer barked at Thorne.

"Hasn't Durrant told you? He knows who I am and why I was there today. Ask your wife. By the way, how is she?" Thorne said coldly.

Singer gave him a curious look and turned to look at Durrant who'd moved away. "Jack, you know this man?" he asked.

"Yes, he was in the hotel at Las Cruces. He was asking questions about the *señora*, and he'd been talking to the livery man about you. He came up from Mexico, that's all I know, boss. His name is Santiago."

"So, you thought you'd waylay the coach, thought it might be carrying something, my wife wearing jewellery," Singer said accusingly.

"If I'd been after the señora's jewellery or money, I'd've had it down in Mexico when those three bandits held up the stage. Wouldn't I, Durrant?" Thorne flung at him. "Your little schemes don't seem to be working out, do they?"

"Shut your filthy mouth. You were

in with those two Federales who came into town yesterday. I guess you shot one of those bandits to make it look good." Durrant shouted, going red in the face.

Singer, looking uncertain now, looked at Thorne. "Santiago, that's Hispanic, Spic, right?"

"I'm an American, Singer, born and raised here," Thorne told him, with assurance.

"Well, that don't mean you're not Hispanic!" Singer retorted, for something better to say.

"D'you call your wife a Spic?" Thorne asked angrily. He wanted badly to relieve himself. He wished to God Estelle would come and sort things out. But would she, he wondered?

Singer swung round. He was puzzled. "Put him in a loose box. I must go to my wife. I'll deal with him in the morning," he ordered Kugler, and then walked off. He turned and called to Durrant, "Jack, I'll see you later after supper. Go see to that arm."

Kugler grinned. He took Thorne by the arm and bundled him into a loose box and tied him to a ring below the feed rack, giving just enough rope for Thorne to sit down in the straw.

"For God's sake! I need to urinate. I can't with my hands tied behind my back," Thorne protested.

Kugler untied his hands and then retied them in front. "I guess you can pee now, you arrogant turkey," he said chuckling, then he went out slamming the top and bottom doors shut. The stallion next door ran around whinnying and stamping for a while.

Thorne did what he had to do with difficulty then sat down on the straw. The place stank of horse manure and urine, and he felt nauseated. He had slept in worse places though. Oh God, he was tired!

★ ★ ★

Estelle had been undressed, bathed and put to bed by two housemaids who were fond of her. Estelle was always careful not to let them see how mean she could be at times as she wanted them on her side. Her head throbbed, but she knew where she was, and what had happened, up until the coach turned over. She had no idea that Santiago had been brought in, nor that he had been out there. It would seem not, as she hadn't caught a glimpse of him anywhere. He'd got his money and vanished. Well, it had been worth it, she thought, smiling. Why had Danson taken the fork route when he knew Max and the boys would be at Hatch? She couldn't figure it, unless Durrant had seen followers. Someone had shot Danson. She must see Durrant and find out before Max came questioning her. What if Durrant had found out about the package de Silva had given her, or heard them talking? There was no one she could trust, she thought. Max was so suspicious, always had been. She got out of bed. Where was her travel bag? She felt panicky. If Max went through it — well, she must bluff it out, somehow.

* * *

Max Singer sat sipping whiskey. "You think this Santiago was after Stell?" he asked Durrant.

"Oh sure, he fancied her right from the start."

"And Stell? How did she — well, did she encourage him?" Singer asked watching Durrant closely.

Durrant answered cautiously. "I can't say really, boss. Women like to be paid a lot of attention. You know that."

"Well, she's fiery, and him being one of her people . . . When I look at some of these frontier women — by God, Jack, I'd sooner have my horses. But these Spanish aristocrats, so called, they got their ways with 'em."

"What you going to do about Santiago? He's been running guns to Varig. You know how Estelle feels about Mexico. If you let him go she might try asking him to help somehow. Best he was out of the picture." Durrant encouraged the thought that he knew was in Singer's mind.

"He must have killed Danson. What if he — oh, go to bed. Leave it until I've talked with Stell," Singer told Durrant. Something, he thought, wasn't quite right. Had Stell been trying to get away from him?

"OK, boss. It ain't no skin off my nose. I'd shoot the bastard, if I was you," Durrant said and finishing his whiskey got up and left the room. "Stupid old sod," he muttered to himself.

Singer was tired, his head ached. He went to bed after looking in on Estelle who was feigning sleep.

★ ★ ★

It was sun-up when the doors were opened and light came into the loose box. An old Mexican stood staring in at

Thorne. He called to him, "You bring water — *agua, por favor?*"

"*Si, si, agua.*" The man ran off and came back with a gourd and held it to Thorne's lips. He drank some down and it was good. The man left the gourd and shot off quickly, and suddenly Kugler appeared in the doorway. "Damned Spic," he said and came and picked up the gourd and poured out the water, grinning nastily.

"So, what do you prefer, Heini's?" said Thorne scathingly, knowing he was asking for it.

"Shut your mouth," Kugler barked, kicking him on the leg, and Thorne winced. "You better not talk to Herr Singer like that or he'll string you up and whip you raw, and then he'll kill you."

"Yeah, well, he probably enjoys that sort of thing. Will he flay his wife when he finds out about Durrant?" Thorne threw back at him, then regretted it. Perhaps Singer would.

Kugler gave him a sharp look. "Just

keep it up, greaser, just you keep it up!" he snarled.

"Durrant killed Danson. You'd better watch out or you'll be next, and the boss, then he'll have it all. He won't want you around," Thorne stirred it.

Kugler gave him another kick then went out closing the doors with a bang and started the stallion, Satan, running round again, and squealing. "Shut up, you mad devil," Kugler yelled at it.

Thorne lay feeling hungry and helpless. The water had helped, but he surely was in an awful predicament.

★ ★ ★

Estelle jumped as the bedroom door opened and Durrant slipped in. He saw she was awake and came and sat on the bed. "You all right?" he asked.

"I've felt a lot better. For God's sake!" — she crossed herself quickly — "what happened? Why did we leave the trail?"

"It was Santiago. He got to Danson,"

Durrant lied. "He's tied up in a loose box. Max wants to talk to you first before he does anything. I said he'd been in Mexico and was probably a federale agent. Might be for all we know."

"Where is the coach driver? I was knocked out so I don't know anything," Estelle said anxiously.

"He's dead. Someone shot him," Durrant said. "I think Santiago killed Fred. Max won't let that go, he liked him."

Estelle said no more, she was still confused. "My travel bag, have you seen it?" she changed the subject.

"I guess Max has it."

"Oh God, then he'll find . . . I mean I need it."

"Listen," said Durrant, leaning over and taking her chin between his fingers. "Don't say anything about me. I tried to help you. If you do I might have to tell Max about that de Silva fella. You *comprende* my dear?"

Estelle winced. "I won't say anything,"

she whispered. "Why should I, Jack? We'll just have to think up some other way. He'll never let me go off again, alone."

"Just leave it awhile. It's best that Santiago dies. He'll only make trouble if Max lets him go," Durrant told her.

"Yes, it must be so. You'd better go now before anyone comes. And Jack, don't come again. Erich might not like it," Estelle said, relishing Durrant's show of angry displeasure.

Durrant got up and left the room. Her threats meant nothing, but Erich Kugler was another matter. One day he would kill that monster. Who the hell cared about her, he could get a dozen like her, if he could get his hands on what she had in that valise. Estelle did not know he'd been watching when de Silva had given her the package, he was sure he'd heard emeralds mentioned.

7

MAX SINGER hadn't slept well and he was not in a good mood after seeing his wife. She had told him how Santiago had followed her from Mexico. She had also told him she thought Danson had been in cahoots with him and possibly the coach driver too. She had not been sure about Jack — though he'd been strange of late. Could Durrant have shot Fred? Santiago is no common man, Singer was thinking. He knows Varig. So, why would he want to rob stages? There had to be more to it. Estelle had told him to do what he thought best and remained in bed, pleading a headache. She had asked for her travel bag. He went through to the kitchen and told Maria, Estelle's maid, to take it up to her, then he went out to look at his horses.

When the bag arrived, and she had dismissed Maria, she emptied it. Wrapped up inside her corset which was again wrapped in a nightdress, she found the silver candlestick. Under the short piece of used candle was a long thin sack containing some large emeralds which had been part of a necklace. She also found four diamonds. Her mother had given them to Don Diego de Silva to pass on to her so she could buy her way to Venezuela. To have trusted Diego was a risk but her mother knew he would do almost anything for Estelle, having been in love with her for years, in fact, since they were very young. She put the candlestick inside a small case in which there were other small items of value, locked it and hid it on a shelf in her wardrobe. If only she could have convinced Santiago to help her get away. What an *hombre*. Durrant she no longer trusted, he was devious beyond measure. She wished now she had put a larger dose in his coffee in

Las Cruces and got rid of him. The doctor had been a fool, he hadn't even considered Durrant might have been poisoned. Well, now she must await another opportunity, and she must get into that bureau and see what Max had in there. To have tried getting to Vera Cruz on her own would have been too dangerous when she was in Mexico, and Diego had taken a risk in coming to find her. She would bide her time and find someone to help her get to one of the Texas ports.

★ ★ ★

Singer stood in front of Thorne who was now on his feet and showing a nasty bruise on his cheek. He had been brought a plate of mush for breakfast which Thorne had told Kugler looked like pig food. Kugler had given him a hard knuckle blow and laughed.

"Before I decide what to do with you," said Singer, "I want your version of yesterday's attack on my wife's coach, and why. A gun-runner don't need to rob stages — not unless he thinks the occupants are carrying something special like jewellery or silver. Perhaps you were just after my wife. So talk — you only have one chance."

Durrant was hovering behind Singer and Kugler straining to hear what was being said.

"Send your two men away, and I'll tell you," Thorne replied.

Singer flushed. "You are in no position to give me orders. Say your piece, or I'll make sure you talk fast enough. Just why were you following the coach? Who sent you?"

"Nobody sends me anywhere, Singer. I'm my own man. Your wife asked me for help. She was afraid. If I were you I'd be more careful who I send as her escorts in future," Thorne said, glaring at Jack Durrant who was looking uneasy.

"You shot Danson to keep him quiet. My wife says the two of you were in it together. So don't lie to me," Singer shouted at Thorne.

"Well, I guess there is no more to be said as whatever I say, you'll still believe what you want to. You're questioning the wrong man. I'd watch your back if I were you, Singer," Thorne said acidly.

Singer struck him across the face with a leather riding crop. Thorne drew in his breath sharply.

"If you think I'm a robber, why haven't you sent for a sheriff? You kill me, you're a murderer," Thorne said, feeling blood trickle down his face.

"I don't need a sheriff. I dispense justice around here. No one will know or care about you, Santiago," Singer, red in the face, shouted back at him.

"Killing a federal agent is a criminal offence," Thorne flung at him desperately.

Singer was momentarily nonplussed. He turned and walked out, almost knocking Durrant off his feet. "Jack, search that arrogant son-of-a-bitch and bring to me every thing you find on him, everything," he said through clenched teeth.

Kugler held Thorne while Durrant emptied his pockets throwing everything into his hat.

"Don't forget the saddle-bags," Thorne said, glowering. He was playing for time. Now they'd be wondering. He had, in fact, sent a lot of information to a certain general he knew in Texas, about the situation in the parts of Mexico he had travelled in. Kept his eyes open as instructed.

After Durrant and Singer had gone through the saddle-bags, in which there was mainly clean underwear, a shirt and toilet bag, a knife, a soggy sandwich, and a handmade map showing the trails to Belen where the ostler had told Thorne the rail tracks were or should be down to by now, they turned to the other items strewn on the kitchen table. There was a timepiece, not worth much. Durrant scoffed. Thorne, being a careful man, having been brought up so by his grandparents, had left the gold watch belonging to his grandpa Hasler, with the other items of value at his bank in Washington. "There's not a damned thing here says who he is," Durrant said frustratedly.

Singer had opened the wallet and found the $100 note and about thirty-five in smaller bills. He found the note written by Estelle, recognizing the writing at once. He thrust it with the dollars into a pocket. "Well, that don't tell us anything," he said.

Estelle who had been too inquisitive and restless to stay in bed, came sauntering in looking somewhat drawn. Durrant, she noticed, looked extremely jumpy.

She had heard Max's comments and seen the articles on the table. She poured a coffee and sat down at the end of the table, looking uninterested, though she was anything but, having suddenly wondered if Santiago had kept her note in his pocket.

Max looked at her, studying her face.

"Santiago says he's a federal agent," he told her.

She looked alarmed for a moment, then shrugged. "He has to say something. Perhaps I can get him to talk," she said blandly.

Singer was still regarding her closely. There was something stinking, he thought. He too had noticed Durrant's edginess. He knew nothing about him really. Durrant, he thought, was very deep. Never said much, whereas Erich, he could read like a book. Erich would do anything for him; he was a brutish, slow-witted man. It was hard to figure just what had been going on. Estelle, he knew, was not happy with him. She had used him, just like he had used her. Well, she'd not had a lot of choice really. Don Artura Benevides had owed him, and he had also been a fool. Perhaps this Santiago was trying to get Estelle away from him to join her mother and sister, wherever they might be. Another thing, her bag had been on the ground near the coach.

103

Why was that? Surely it would have been inside when the coach went over? It had come to him this morning while he was mulling things over. He could not trust anyone, Durrant knew more than he was saying. Perhaps he and Fred had been in cahoots. Santiago had hinted as much. Fred had always been loyal though.

Durrant took himself off again when Estelle arrived. He didn't trust the bitch. She'd used him, just like that fool Santiago. Perhaps he should just ride on out. He went to his room at the rear of the house and lay on his bed, his arm was throbbing, and he cursed.

Max Singer looked at his wife. "I don't want you going near that man," he told her.

"Are you going to kill him?" she asked, looking dispassionately down the table. She regretted now her dalliance with Santiago. It had all gone wrong because of him, she thought, illogically. What if he was a Mexican agent? What could they want with her now?

"I don't think so, Stell. I don't know what's been going on. Jack is like a Mexican jumping bean, and that ain't like him."

"You think he killed Fred? I don't know where he was when the coach tipped over. He decided to ride. He was supposed to be watching out for those two men."

"I'll find out what it was all about," Singer said. "It's amazing what a bull-whip can get a man to say."

Estelle ate little at midday. She hated Max and his brutish ways. He was no better than those fiends in Mexico who dragged men to their deaths, or lashed them to pulp, just for sport. She went back to her bedroom, wishing she could pay someone to let Santiago go, but they would all be too scared, and Kugler would not do anything against Max, he was a dirty sneak, that one.

★ ★ ★

105

Thorne was worried and feeling light-headed. The stink of horse urine made him nauseated. His stomach was empty. He wondered where Crenna was, hoped he was keeping out of sight. It would do no good for him to get caught.

Singer had drunk a fair amount of whiskey when he came, carrying a bull-whip. He belched loudly as Erich Kugler dragged Thorne out into the yard. "Tie him to the coach wheel," Singer told the big man. "Now we see what he is made of." He had read the note from Estelle to Santiago, at least four times. So, they had been lovers. He would see how Estelle would react when she heard his whimpering.

Thorne had a desire to urinate when he saw that Singer had been drinking. His face and piggy eyes were red, and sweat ran down his face. Kugler tore his shirt apart and pushed him against the coach wheel. "Now, I enjoy this, you greaser pig," he said into Thorne's ear.

Thorne felt real fear. He would

rather they just shot him and be done with it. He tried to turn his head. "Hey, Singer, you afraid to do your own dirty work," he called out. Singer, he felt was not so powerful as the big yellow-haired bastard.

Singer, who had passed the whip to Kugler, flushed deeply. There were some wranglers, Durrant and the old yardman, watching. A look of fury spread over his face as he took the whip from Kugler, who looked sulkily disappointed.

The whip came down hard, it was stranded at the end and bit into Thorne's skin; he almost bit through his lips. The old man stepped forward and put a piece of thong between his teeth. Singer glowered at him and he stepped back and went to lean against the wall where the stallion was snorting, his head over the door. Timo's father had been Spanish, his mother Isleta Indian. He had seen many cruel things in his time, and borne a great deal of unutterable hardship. He hated Singer, and soon he would leave this place. Worst of all, he hated the big yellow-haired gringo.

It was at the sixth lash that rifle shots stopped the procedure. Everyone stood like statues for a moment, then Durrant called out, "Round the front, boss," and ran out through the arch, the others after him.

Singer strode hastily into the house to fetch his rifle. Kugler yanked his side-gun as he ran to an iron gate, opened it, and ran on through a passage to the front garden.

When Estelle had left her room and crossed the corridor, going into another room that overlooked the inner yard, and watched her husband bring down the whip on Santiago, she almost cried out. Max would kill that beautiful man who'd made real love to her. It was better a bullet than that. She must do something. Rushing back to her room she took a rifle from the wardrobe which Max had taught her to shoot when they'd first come to the hacienda and Indians were about. She levered it, went on to her balcony and made several shots into the air, then she went out running along the corridor and down the stairs. The yard was empty when she ran out there. Timo, she saw was hurriedly pouring water into Thorne's mouth from a goatskin. She ran across quickly. "Don't let the *patron* see you," she told the old man. "*Madre de Dios*! Santiago. Why don't you tell him what he wants to know?" She looked into the puffed up face.

Thorne who was close to passing out said feebly, "Why don't you tell him the truth, that Durrant is a killer — probably your lover." His head sank down.

Estelle went pale, she heard footsteps coming from the passageway, and Kugler with Max came into the yard.

"Get away from him," Singer yelled. "What are you doing?" He came forward and thrust her out of the way.

"I heard shots. I thought I saw

someone out in the scrub. He must have friends. Perhaps those two from Mexico. Federales," she said, breathlessly.

"Get him back inside," Singer told Kugler angrily.

"Max, do not do this cruel thing. It is barbaric," Estelle cried out and ran on back to the house.

Singer stood looking after her, an expression of pure frustration upon his face. He picked up the whip and followed her. If he threw her out everyone would laugh at him. Jan Steiner would say, I told you so. He would be a laughing stock. Perhaps he should let Santiago go. He could not afford to have the law coming snooping around. Yes, he would let him go, the insolent bastard. What if he should be an agent for the government? Kugler could rough him up some more, that would warn him off.

8

P AT CRENNA had been watching
the hacienda through the spyglass
all morning from his hiding place
next to a prickly pear. He had seen a
couple of *vaqueros* ride westward to
where several steers were grazing. At
the side of the outer buildings four
men were working with some horses
in a large corral. At a smaller corral
he had detected Single amongst other
horses, but so far he had seen no sign
of Santiago. He wished he knew what
was going on and where they had him
located.

The big yellow-haired bruiser had
taken him and Pat feared that if the
señora's husband let that one loose
on Santi, he'd kill him. The heat was
beating down on Pat and he was so
hungry his stomach felt quite flat. He'd
had nothing but water since stopping at

111

the way-station yesterday. How far it was to Hatch he could only speculate. Possibly around ten miles. He daren't leave until he had found out what they'd done with Santiago. They had taken the two dead men and he'd seen a couple of Mexicans digging over by a stand of trees. Perhaps he could speak to one of them, give him a dollar and ask him a few questions. It would be best to wait until dark, but that was a long way off. As far as he could see he was safe enough where he was and the horse well hidden. There wasn't much else he could do but rest.

★ ★ ★

Thorne could hear some activity in the yard. If they came for him again, he doubted he would last long. He'd been near to fainting last time. His back was extremely sore and the straw irritated the weals. He had soiled his pants when he was beaten and his own stench made him feel sick. What a damned fool he'd been to let that woman involve him in her game, whatever it was. He could hear voices then a wagon moving. "Leave it at the livery in Hatch," he heard Durrant tell someone.

The doors opened and Durrant came in. "Well, Santiago, how do you feel now?" he asked, coming over to look down on him, a smug look on his face.

"How d'you think, you murdering scum?" Thorne retorted, his voice hoarse.

"You never give up, do you, you stupid idiot? Anyway, I have a proposition for you. It's Saturday and most of the men are going into town, Kugler too. If I got your horse and left it under those trees outside the gate and distracted the guard on duty, then cut you free, are you fit enough to ride?"

Thorne didn't answer for a moment. He was thinking hard. "I might be. Why should you let me go? Singer would kill you."

"He'd not know it was me. I could

113

say it was the guard."

"And he'd be shot, or whipped to death. You're a cold-blooded bastard, Durrant," Thorne said angrily.

"He could ride off with you. Juan Vegas, a *vaqueros* will do anything for a few bucks."

"I'll think about it," said Thorne.

"It'll be your only chance, believe me. The *señora* won't help you," Durrant told him and went out closing the doors. A few minutes later Timo came in with a glass of milk and a ham sandwich. He had also brought Santiago's clean shirt which he figured Durrant must have had. He probably had his boots too which had cost quite a lot of dough.

"*Muchas gracias*," Thorne told him.

"*Por nada, señor*," said the old man and departed.

Thorne sat thinking as he drank some milk with difficulty. His face was swollen and his back was on fire, every movement brought an agony. Durrant was up to something, he believed.

Perhaps Estelle had sent the food. He ate every morsel and finished the milk. It would give him strength. He had quite expected to have been shot by now. Perhaps Singer did believe he was a government agent. He obviously didn't want to hand him over to the law, so what had he to hide? It might be that he was just vindictive, a sadist. Oh hell! Estelle's note, he must have read it. Heaven help Estelle, if he had. It had been in his pocket. Maybe Singer would use it to torment her. He was obviously not sure what had been going on with Durrant and Danson.

It had been dark for some time, but Thorne wasn't sure how far on the evening was. He'd heard horses leaving and men laughing. He hadn't seen the big one since morning nor Durrant. Timo had removed the glass and plate and left water in the gourd. He had also produced a cigar and some matches.

★ ★ ★

The Mexican on guard at the barn was seated on an upturned bucket, smoking and muttering to himself. Suddenly a hand slid round from behind and clamped down on his mouth. "Don't move or I will hurt you," a voice told him. "You *comprende*?"

"*Si, comprende*," said Felipe Santander. He was not about to argue with a piece of sharp steel close to his face.

"Where have they got the big gringo, Santiago." Crenna asked him.

"Inside, *señor*," squawked Santander.

"Inside where? He is not a prisoner?"

"*Si, prisionero*. In *caballa casa*."

Crenna said, "You give poncho, hat; I give dollar." He pulled the poncho off Santander and then moved him in behind some bins and tied him up with rope. Then he took the sombrero and put on the poncho after stuffing a bandanna into the Mexican's mouth, and sauntered out, keeping his hand on his six-gun under the poncho. He was wearing some moccasins he'd once taken from a Sioux, and which he kept in his saddle-bags. He could see the dark form of the guard leaning on the gate. Going quickly, he slipped to the door which he noticed was closed at the top. Most others were open as the nights were not yet very cold. He opened the top part and leaning in called softly, "Santi, you in there?"

Thorne, who was sitting dozing, propped by the top of his shoulders which had not been hit by the whip. He lifted his head. "Pat?" he whispered.

Crenna climbed in over the door then closed the top part and felt his way over. He thumbed a match into light. "Oh Jeezus! What they done to you, Santi?" he gasped, anger rising in him.

Thorne almost smiled but couldn't. "That big one, the bastard, he likes to rough people up. It was Singer though who used the whip."

"Can you walk?"

"Not well. I have no boots. They took everything. Durrant actually sent me a fresh shirt, my own. I got some food this afternoon. He said he would help me get away tonight. I don't trust him. Christ, he shot Danson in the back. He told Singer, Danson and I were in on it together. In on what?"

"Durrant, as you call him, shot that driver. He was out cold in the bush."

"I think they're looking for an excuse to shoot me," said Thorne dejectedly.

"I could get you away now. I've seen Single in a corral. I'd have to carry you over there."

"There must be guards all about," Thorne said. "I told Singer I'm a federal agent and I'm not alone. That'll make him think. I told him about Durrant but I guess Durrant has denied everything. Hey, there was gunfire just when Singer was wielding his whip. They took off. I believe it saved me."

"I heard it and saw men running about. I thought you must have escaped. Listen, I've got a greaser tied up in the barn, this is his poncho. If I get another you could wear it. We could get away."

"Pat, like I said, I don't want your death on my conscience. If you could go find a sheriff perhaps."

"I thought on it. I even thought about writing Singer a note, only I don't write good," Crenna said.

"Ssh! There's somebody coming, get under the straw quick," Thorne whispered fearfully.

The top door came open. A soft voice called out, "Santiago, are you all right?" Estelle enquired.

"What do you think? Perhaps we could do a fandango together," said Thorne bitterly.

"Ah Santiago, if only we could! Listen, I think Max will let you go tomorrow. He is afraid there may be questions. I told him a lot of people in Las Cruces are acquainted with you. I will always remember my night in Las Cruces, such a special place, *mi querido*. I must go. *Adios*," she said hurriedly.

Thorne could hear her speaking but could not make out what was said.

She had left the top door open and he could see the night was bright with moonlight.

A form appeared at the doorway. "Been saying your fond farewells, Santiago," Durrant called out. "You should've taken my offer. You'd better say your beads *amigo* tomorrow at dawn . . . " Durrant didn't finish, he just laughed harshly and closed both doors.

Crenna crawled out and got close to Thorne. "Now you know. She says one thing and him another. Who do you trust?" asked Crenna.

"Neither!" said Thorne. Their perfidy turned his stomach.

"Seems like you was a naughty boy in Las Cruces, Santi. Didn't I always tell you when we were in Mexico, watch out for the *señoras* and especially the *señoritas*?"

"If I recall, you spent your time running after them," Thorne said gruffly.

"Ah yes, but I always leave them

happy and move on. No female is ever going to put her stamp on me," said Crenna. "Especially now!"

Thorne knew what he was intimating. He said, "you'd best get going. Someone is bound to find that guard," he told Crenna, worriedly.

"I can get you away. Here I've got a knife. You keep it. Most of the men have gone to town, and these Mex fellas aren't too alert, they don't care."

"Here, take my hat, there is something inside the inner band. If I don't get away, you have it," Thorne said, and got up slowly to take the hat out of the hay rack where it had been thrown. "Now go!"

Crenna was gone and the door shut as someone came walking through the archway. Pat was crouched near a potted plant, and as soon as he saw the big fella disappear he ran to the barn and slid in silently. He untied the Mexican, gave him three dollars. "I keep poncho and sombrero," he told him. Santander grinned and snatched it quickly. "You not tell," Crenna told him. "The gringo, he *bueno hombre*, he *mi amigo*! He do *nada*!"

Santander nodded and Crenna was gone quickly. He ran to the corral and lifting a bridle off a rail went in and found Single. "They ain't getting you," Crenna told the horse who nuzzled him and nickered. Suddenly there was a pounding of hoofs and about six *vaqueros* came riding across to the corral. "Damn," said Crenna and slipped out at the back, leaving the bridle and crawled away on his belly to find cover. A couple of the men stood smoking and talking, so he had to abandon his plan to take Single. When he got back to his hideout he was fuming. Somehow he'd get those bastards who'd beaten up Santi, he vowed.

★ ★ ★

Kugler went in to see Max Singer after he had spoken with Durrant. "You OK boss?" he asked, he could see Singer was pretty drunk. "Why don't you go to bed? You look all in."

"I was about to. Did the boys get the coach back to the livery all right?" Singer asked gruffly.

"Sure, the stage-line say they want fifty bucks for the damage and for extra time. They was asking about the driver. I said he had left after you paid him," Kugler told Singer, grinning broadly.

"Good! I still think it was a silly idea hiring it, they could have come on the normal coach."

"Yeah, well I think it was Durrant's idea. You shouldn't trust him boss. I think he got ideas about your *frau*," said Kugler maliciously.

"I don't trust nobody, Erich," said Singer. "I've made a decision. Before it gets light I want you to put that turkey on to his horse and put him off my place. I don't want government or Mexican agents coming here snooping around. You keep an eye on Durrant for me, too."

"And the *frau*?"

"I said Durrant. I'll look after my wife," Singer said sharply. "You do exactly as I say, Erich."

"Yes, boss," Kugler said and went out. He headed for the bunkhouse he shared with the wranglers. Most of them ignored him, they all knew what a dangerous sneak he was.

9

THORNE stirred when the door opened suddenly. It was cold and not yet light. What now? Was this it? Kugler came over. "Get up; *schnell*!" he snapped and kicked Thorne in the ribs.

"*Jawohl*!" Thorne responded, he just couldn't help it. He got to his feet, and Kugler stared at the clean shirt, but made no comment. The damned *frau* he was thinking. "The boss say to let you go," he told Thorne and untied the rope from the ring.

"What about my boots, my other things?" Thorne asked as he struggled to stay upright.

Kugler leered. "The boss say nothing about your things. I do as he say." He led Thorne through the archway stumbling along on hard stony ground. His feet were all bruised by the time they got to the barn where Kugler left him sitting on a grain bin. "You move before I come back, I kill you," he said snarling into Thorne's face. Thorne didn't think he could move. He sat staring out into the night very suspicious. A shot in the back he thought, while he rode out. He heard a horse coming. Was Singer really letting him go? He felt the knife that Crenna had given him hanging down inside his trouser leg on a piece of string. Could he use it on Kugler? Damn it! He had no strength, that big one would crush him to death in minutes.

Kugler came in. "Now, mister smart-ass, I'm going to give you a going away present, you spying son-of-a-spic," he said, smiling. He pulled Thorne up and started hitting him in the gut and ribs. Each time Thorne sank down, he was dragged up again and pushed against a wall while Kugler's big knuckled fists gave him blow after blow.

"What the hell is going on here?" a wrangler's voice came from the doorway, and he strode inside.

"None of your goddamned business," Kugler told him and dragged Thorne out into the open and literally lifted him up like he weighed nothing and flung him on to Single's back. There was no saddle. Thorne fell forward over the horse's neck and Kugler reached for a rope and lashed him down. The horse snorted and moved about and Kugler hit him with the rope. He ran it over Thorne and under the belly several times then tied it off firmly. He then fetched his own horse and after tying a lead-line to Single, went on to the gate where a Mexican guard opened it for him, and threw a nasty comment at Kugler's back.

About two miles along the track to Hatch, Kugler got down and took off the lead-line. Thorne's head was hanging down by the horse's neck and Kugler shouted in his ear, "Don't you never come back. If you do you're a dead man. I'll tear you apart!"

Thorne didn't answer, he'd passed

out; Kugler hit Single across the rump a stinging blow with the line and he shot off along the trail at a gallop.

Kugler watched while he lit a stogey. He was thinking if the horse didn't get to Hatch it might go anywhere. Could be days before anyone saw it. The bastard would die real slow.

★ ★ ★

Crenna had fetched his horse and was down in a scrape about a mile off the trail to Hatch. He'd caught a jackrabbit by hitting it on the head with a knotted piece of rope. Many times he had killed game that way when he was in the army. The food had been so bad and not much of it, he recalled. That had been one of the reasons he had left. His mother Irish, his father Italian, they'd always had good home-cooked meals. His father's quick temper had driven him from home, but he had his mother's stubbornness in him. He had to get Santiago away tonight, by God. On a low fire he cooked the skinny rabbit and ate the lot ravenously, then drank some water. If he went to find a sheriff, he might find out he was a deserter, and Pat would rather die than be taken to the stockade at Leavenworth. There must be a way. If he started a fire near the stables and one at the barn, he could get Santi out while they were all running around like a lot of headless chickens. Dressed in the poncho he would not be suspected, surely. Damn it! It would work. He grinned then sobered. What if they killed Santi today, before he could do anything. Well, that would be the end of it. Just when he was beginning to really like him. Just who the hell was he though?

The dun suddenly gave a soft nicker and its ears went forward. Pat had a feeling something or someone was out there. It might be cattle. He got up and stamped the fire out and threw dust over it. He cinched up the saddle then eased himself up into it and rode on out moving eastwards to angle for the trail. He might just as well go to take a look at Hatch and get some decent food; there was nothing he could do until it came dark and that was a long way off. A beer would be real nice, he thought.

★ ★ ★

After running about half a mile, Single kept looking round, he could feel Thorne's head at his neck. Something was wrong. He nickered and nothing happened. The horse stood for some time then slowly moved off the track and went down to nibble at some leaves. For a while he snuffed around and plucked at the yellow grasses. He'd had little fodder since leaving Las Cruces. The sun was up and warming the earth and Single worked his way down a declivity. A jackrabbit sprang away and jumped. The rope moved at the front of his belly and eased, the second strand also loosened.

Thorne swung sideways and hung there. His eyes came open. Vaguely he saw the ground below his head. Mother of God, where was he? His whole body was shot through with pain. His head was thumping and hair stuck to his face from the horse's neck. "Single," he called weakly. The horse nickered and looked round and stood still. Thorne got his left hand free and tugged at the rope, prising it forward. He could feel something sticking into his leg that hung round the horse's belly. He remembered the knife and slowly, grinding his teeth at the pain, got a hand inside his trousers and managed to get it out. He sawed at the rope and then suddenly it all gave and he landed on the ground, almost on his head, the knife left his hand catching Single's fetlock and he leapt forward hitting Thorne with a back hoof, and he let out a yell and lay there.

★ ★ ★

Crenna had moved across the track. He was now hell bent on getting to a beer. Why should he help Santi? He'd got himself into his own mess over that damned *señora*. Only a few days ago he was holding a gun on Santi. Could he have killed him though? He had killed Indians, but he'd never killed for fun or vengeance. Santi had given him the money, and half what that female had given him. It was a long time since he'd had over a hundred bucks in his pocket. The dun interrupted his argumentative thoughts as it gave out with a whinny and stepped out anxiously. "Easy boy," said Pat and drew his side-arm. His eyes swept around the scene, then he saw Single. "What the hell!" he uttered. He stepped down from the saddle and went forward leading the dun. Single nickered and Crenna now saw the ropes hanging from his back, and noted there was no saddle. Cautiously he moved forward and right before him he saw the body on the ground. Again he scrutinized every bit of cover to see if he could detect anyone, anything out of place. Satisfied, though still uneasy he went forward to Thorne believing he was dead. Pat put a hand to his neck as he lay on his side, one arm outstretched the other under him, Pat's knife lay a few feet away. There was a pulse. "Holy mother of God!" he exclaimed. "What in hell have they done to you, Santi?" Pat asked. "Hey! Wake up, Santi, it's Patrick."

Thorne stirred, his eyes opened and he tried to push himself up. "My ribs," he cried out.

"Jeez, you're in a fine mess," said Pat. "You got no boots, your pants are all fouled up, you look like one of them drunks you find under a saloon."

"I'm done for, Pat. I can't move."

"No you ain't. You need a doctor real bad. Now I'm gonna put you over there under that bush. I'll take Single with me and get to town fast and bring back a wagon. It'll take a couple of hours maybe," said Crenna. He put

133

his hands under Thorne's shoulders and dragged him gently over and laid him under a bush growing out of the bank. He brought his bedroll and covered him. Then he put his Colt close to Thorne's hand. "Just in case," he said.

"You'll need money," said Thorne feebly.

"I got enough. Who was it done this to you? Did the *señora* get you away? I was coming tonight," Pat said.

"Singer let me go, and that yellow-haired gorilla gave me a going away present."

"One day I'll fix that Heini, so help me," Pat said, his face grim. He got mounted and rode away leading Single, at a fast pace.

10

"AH, now that's better," a warm feminine voice came to Thorne's ears. Where was he? He opened his eyes and saw half-drawn, pretty curtains. A shaft of sunlight hit the whitewashed wall close to his head.

"You'll be wanting something to eat now," the voice said. "After all that sleeping."

"Who are you? Where am I?" Thorne asked seeing only vaguely the rosy-faced woman leaning over him.

"I'm Madge Jackson and I'm a nurse, well, sort of, and you're in Father Brady's house in Hatch. Your friend brought you in yesterday morning."

"Oh," said Thorne. "Patrick, is he here?"

"Well now," Madge said, looking at a fob watch hanging from her cardigan which covered a cotton frock and a wholesome figure. "I think about this time, he'll be at the cantina, it's cheaper he says than the saloon." Madge smiled. "He's been worried about you, he's hardly left your side since he brought you in. I told him to get some air."

"I see," Thorne said and tried to sit up, and yelped. He felt something tight around his middle. "You'd best lie still. You've got broken ribs. Father Brady lent you one of his nightshirts," Madge explained. "There's no doctor in Hatch, it being just a small place, so I do what I can, and Father Brady is as good as some doctors, especially those army ones," said Madge emphatically. "Now I'll go fix you some good thick broth for starters. You stay quiet, it's rest you need."

Thorne lay thinking. It was a miracle he had survived. If Pat hadn't been around he doubted he would have after what Kugler had done to him. Single could have wandered for days and never been spotted. He smouldered with fury. That *schweinhund* — one day I'll fix that sadistic bastard.

After he had eaten Madge's thick vegetable broth Thorne slept again. The pain he had felt when Crenna had found him had eased considerably with help from the laudanum Madge had given him. Physically he felt more comfortable but mentally he could hardly contain his dark thoughts about Singer. How could Estelle have married such a cold-blooded fiend, he wondered?

The door opened and a black-clad priest, with a ruddy complexion, greying hair, about five feet ten, came in. He said cheerily, "I'm glad to see you're improving after Madge's care. She's a fine woman!"

"I'm extremely grateful," Thorne told him. "I guess I'm lucky to be still alive."

"I expect it's the Lord's will," responded Father Brady. "He must have other plans for you, Señor Santiago."

Thorne suppressed a smile. He said nothing to set Father Brady right as to his true identity. Let them think what they wished. Once his ribs were healed he would be heading north to reach the rail tracks.

"Those marks on your back," Father Brady looked at Thorne enquiringly. "What fiend did that to you? May I ask why?"

"You might well ask, Father. Pure sadism I'd say. Then down in Mexico it is done all the time to innocent peons, or dissenters, whatever."

"Mexico, is that where you've been? Yes, it is bad down there, if you get mixed up in politics."

"When I left Mexico I was in good health. No, it wasn't Mexicans who beat me up," Thorne said, leaving Father Brady's questions unanswered.

Keeping his own counsel, Brady did not press the matter. He bid Thorne adieu and said he'd look in later. He had heard that Will Carter's son, Ned, had taken a wagon out somewhere to pick up Santiago, but the lad was keeping his lips closed, which was something of a change. Crenna, he had observed was as closed-up and devious as a government tax collector. So, just what had been going on? Whatever it was, nobody should've beaten Santiago near to death's door like that. He had helped Madge Jackson peel off those stinking clothes and seen the festering weals before she'd dressed them, while Thorne was still unconscious. He had seen many bad things in the Civil War, and folks who'd been tortured by Indians, but what excuse was there now for a man to be treated so, he wondered sadly?

When Pat Crenna arrived, Thorne put on a broad smile. He stretched out a hand and Crenna took it. "I'm truly grateful to you, Pat. You surely saved my life."

"Hell, you saved mine in Mexico a couple of years ago. I don't know what got into me when I tried that stunt when I followed you from El Paso.

I guess I was just plain loco. I was jealous, you looking so prosperous, an' all I had was a couple of bucks."

"It's no matter," Thorne told him. "Life is — well, things happen sometimes."

"How're you feeling now?"

"Much better. Mrs Jackson is a remarkable woman. How did you discover her?"

"Oh, the lad at the livery who I got the wagon from. He helped me bring you in. Madge is all they got here. Ned said she once had to cut a fella's leg off on account it'd gone gangrenous. I reckon she's as good as any Doc. I ain't told them nothing. I give the kid two bucks to keep his trap shut. I kinda told him he'd better."

Thorne laughed. "With those two front teeth missing you'd scare the Devil," he said.

Crenna's face darkened. "Madge sez same as you done, I can get two fixed in there with a special dentist. Where the hell am I going to find one, or the dough?" Pat said miserably.

Looking contrite, Thorne said, "You never know. I've got an idea, but first I want to be on my feet again. Are you staying around, Pat?"

"I got nothing better to do. You gonna run some more guns. I could help?"

"No, I'm finished with that. Hand me my hat will you?" Thorne asked Crenna.

Crenna picked it off a chair, watching Thorne. He had looked inside the inner band after taking it before. He had seen the folded money and an envelope but had not touched it. Thorne peeled off a $100 note. "Here, go get me some pants, another shirt, and some boots and a jacket, and take what you paid out for the wagon. Tomorrow I'm out of this bed. I can sit in a chair. Is there a hotel?"

"Beaver's rooming-house, is all," Crenna said.

"You get two rooms there tomorrow, for a week. It might be dangerous for

Mrs Jackson if I stay here. Where are you at now?"

"At the livery. Madge ain't going to be pleased if you leave that bed yet."

"Well, she has no say in it. She can come visit me each day, I'll pay her."

"Sure, Santi, if you say so," Crenna said grinning. He pocketed the money. It sure was lucky Singer and Kugler never thought of looking in that hat and that he'd gotten it away.

"Oh, Pat," called Thorne, "stay off the pulque. I want you sharp."

When Thorne told Madge about his plans, she wasn't happy. "You shouldn't be out of bed for another week," she told him. Madge enjoyed looking after people.

★ ★ ★

Pat Crenna was up in the hay loft sleeping off last evening's session at the Barn Door Saloon where he'd lifted a jar or two with two mule-skinners, when he heard voices below.

Someone was questioning Ned. Pat moved forward on his belly and peered down. He drew in his breath sharply when he saw Durrant who had Ned up against a roof post. "This fella who brought that man in on Sunday. Who is he? Is he still in town? You better answer, boy," Durrant snapped.

"I don't know, honest. I ain't seen him since. He could be in the cantina. The other fella is at Madge Jackson's, that's all I know."

Durrant let Ned go and went on out. Crenna called down. "Hey, Ned, what time is it?"

"Near to eleven. You hear that?"

"Sure. Thanks Ned. That man's a killer. You stay clear of him, you hear?" Crenna called down. He went on down and cleaned himself up at the water trough. Then he fetched a parcel from the tack room and went off across a tiny square to Madge Jackson's house which was situated not far from the small church and Father Brady's cabin. He went in the rear door and found Madge putting a cake into the oven. "Did Santi tell you he's removing himself to the rooming-house?" he asked her.

"Yes, he did," Madge said, aggrieved. He could see she was real put out.

"Well it's best. He don't want to bring no trouble on yer. And if you got a yen for him, he sez you can visit him there."

Madge Jackson smiled. "Now if I was twenty years younger," she sighed.

And then some, Crenna thought. "I brung him some new clothes. I'll go get him ready," he told her.

By the time Thorne was settled into his room he was wringing with sweat. Damn it! he thought. It's going to take time before I'm fit. He could see that Crenna was nervous. "What is it, Pat? You seem edgy this morning? You thinking of leaving?"

"No, I ain't leaving. It's just that — well, that Durrant fella was in the livery this morning asking Ned Carter a lot of questions about the man who helped bring you in on Sunday."

"He's probably trying to find out about me. He would see Single in the livery barn. They found out quick."

"Sure, an' there's plenty who will tell Durrant where you're at for a whiskey or two."

"Well I hope that gorilla doesn't come into town. Durrant will want to know if you're another government agent. I think I scared them about that. They must have something to hide I'm thinking. If that bastard goes near Madge or Brady, I'll kill him," Thorne said, beginning to sweat again.

★ ★ ★

Max Singer was standing next to a tall, dark-haired man dressed in black broadcloth jacket, cord britches and long boots. "They're fine horses, Singer," said Frank Turner, a newcomer living near Deming, a town where the SP railroad was about to reach, and from where the two horses would be transported to California. Turner passed over $400 to Singer and he in turn gave a sales slip to him, smiling broadly. "You tell your friends I have some more young stock, they'll be ready in about four months. My men can bring them to you at Deming."

"Splendid. I'll put the word out," Turner said and turned to an elderly Mexican holding a big roan gelding and an Appaloosa. They each took a lead line and rode away taking the two greys with them.

Estelle sat in the big living-room as her husband came in humming to himself; his walk was brisk. She watched him open up the bureau and put the money into a box, then he locked it, and the bureau, putting the key back on to his watch chain. How she would love to get into that bureau. Just how much cash, and what else had he in there? Before the Federales had taken her father and brother away, her father had told her where to find money and emeralds he had hidden. Max had taken them off her later when they had come to the hacienda, saying he would look after them. Arturo Benevides had trusted Max Singer, they'd been friends in South America before coming to Mexico. He had encouraged Singer in the marriage with his daughter when he became afraid of events in Mexico. Max would look after her, if anything should happen to him; she was his favourite of his three children. Her mother had been afraid that day when Max, three years ago, had come to tell them her father had been arrested. Carlos had got away but had been caught later. Max had arranged for her mother and Maria to get away from Mexico City, and then taken Estelle north and into America. Later she had discovered the Austrian helping her mother and sister had left them. It had taken months to find out where they were hiding. Her mother had warned her about Max. Don't trust him she had said as they'd exchanged their goodbyes. Now she knew what a devil he was.

At first he had charmed her, then after the marriage he had changed. Only occasionally a letter had come from her mother, saying they were moving again. It was after that last letter had arrived that she had persuaded Max to let her go and try to see them, try to help. It had been a journey in vain except for the meeting with Diego; he had set her straight on how Max had betrayed her father. It was after that meeting that Durrant had suggested he help her to get away. It had seemed a good idea at first until Durrant had become too familiar. She'd been afraid and played along with him, and it had given her an idea.

"You sold the horses, I see," she said.

"*Ja*, I sold them. Turner has rich friends in California. He will tell them about my horses," said Singer rubbing his hands together.

"Why don't we sell up and go to California? It is so boring here, so quiet. Nowhere to go," Estelle wailed, watching Max closely.

"You know why. I got no papers. One day I get. I don't want to be put back over the border," Max snapped. "Nobody find me here."

"Lots of people have no papers," Estelle replied.

"Nobody worry about greasers, they work cheap. One day we go to California. I buy papers when I get right connections. First you give me a son so I got somebody to leave my land to. Land will be worth plenty money one day. You'll see," Singer told Estelle, tossing back a large whiskey. "Come," he went over and pulled her out of the chair. "Now we go upstairs. I buy you present when I go to Las Cruces, soon maybe."

Estelle pulled back. "You haven't had your lunch," she said.

Singer slapped her hard. "Enough with the excuses. How long you think I wait?" he pulled her through the door and up the stairs. "You sleep with that Santiago — you *puta*," he snarled at her.

Estelle bit back her anger and her tears. Now I will kill this pig soon. Somehow I do it, she vowed.

Kugler, who'd been standing behind a large plant, a lascivious smirk on his face was chuckling inanely. Now the boss would fix that bitch good.

11

WHEN Durrant got back to the hacienda he was whistling. He winked at one of the housemaids whom he sometimes had a tumble with for half a dollar. "Where's the jefe?" he asked her. The girl pointed upstairs and made a rude gesture. Durrant passed on to his room. Poor Estelle. Why the hell she had married an old stud like Singer he couldn't comprehend. Then he supposed it was for a better life out of Mexico. He lit a cigar and threw himself on to his bed. What would Santiago do when he recovered, he wondered? That bastard Kugler must've given him a real going over before he strapped him down on the horse. It was lucky for Santiago that the horse was found, or he'd surely be dead by now. One of the wranglers had told him about how he'd come upon Kugler in the barn. Even if Singer knew about it, he'd do nothing, probably congratulate that big dumb idiot.

It was Santander who'd mentioned that Santiago had had a visit in the loose box, as Timo had let it slip. Santander had now ridden out. Soon they'd all be going. Singer did not inspire any loyalty, that was sure. Soon he would haul his freight too.

About 6.30 Durrant went into the house to make his report. Singer was sitting with a large whiskey in his hand. There was a dark mark near his left eye and Jack figured Estelle must have given him it. It would not be the first time. Max was in a foul mood, he could see. He helped himself to a whiskey, a privilege no other employee had been allowed, and it galled Erich Kugler who had walked out as Jack came in.

"So, what did you find out?" asked Singer.

"Santiago is in Hatch at Father

Brady's place. Someone borrowed a wagon on Sunday and brought him in. He was in a hell of a mess, broken ribs and had been strapped to his horse, so I heard."

"A wagon? What happened to the horse? Why was he strapped to it?"

"You might well ask that gorilla of yours. You should get rid of that one, Max," said Durrant. He got up and closed the door and then sat next to Singer. "Santander told me all about it, he's ridden out. Maybe there'll be more leaving. That horse could have wandered for days; Santiago would have died. Not that I'm bothered about that, but there's folks as might ask what is going on."

Singer swore a string of oaths in Austrian. "Erich always overdoes it. I'll speak to him," was all he said to Durrant.

"If someone done that to me I'd be pressing charges with the sheriff. You should have shot Santiago and got rid of his horse."

"I make the mistake. I didn't want the law out here. There's something about this Santiago. Erich says he speaks German. We'd better keep an eye on him."

"Why don't you send Estelle in? I reckon she could find out what Santiago is up to," Durrant said, watching Singer closely. "Where is she, boss?"

"She's got a headache. You can join me for supper if you like. You take her to town tomorrow."

Surprised, Durrant poured himself another drink. Just why was Singer so afraid of the law, he wondered? He suddenly remembered a comment Carl Sneider had once made when they were drinking in the Barn Door Saloon, about Singer's predecessor Stanton, a widower. He'd supposedly gone back East after selling to Max, to get treatment for an illness. Durrant sweated, he had an uneasy feeling, his thoughts were dark.

★ ★ ★

It was about 11 a.m. next morning, and Madge Jackson had just left Thorne's room after checking his back and taking him more laudanum, when there was a knock on his door. Thorne went to open it and was astonished to find Estelle Singer standing there. She was dressed in a smart riding outfit. She smiled, the sort of smile she'd used in Las Cruces, and for a second he felt a shiver run through him. "Estelle, you!" he spluttered. "How on earth did you know where to find me?"

"Not difficult, Santiago! You're hot news around town, I gather. Father Brady told me," she said.

"You'd better come in," Thorne said, looking anything but pleased. His body ached all over. "I'm surprised Singer let you come to town, or did he send you?" he asked coldly.

Estelle's eyes for a moment went hard. She sat on the chair he offered her, glancing around the room which was rather spartan. "Jack brought me in. Max is busy with his horses. When

I heard how that pig Erich treated you. My God!" — she crossed herself — "Max should get rid of him, but he feels some sort of duty towards him. I don't know why."

"Well, Kugler almost finished me off, but it was your husband who used the bull-whip. He enjoyed it I'm sure," Thorne responded, heatedly. "Just what is it you want, Estelle?" he asked.

Flushing deeply, Estelle replied, "Nothing, I — er, I was worried about you," she said meekly.

"You weren't much help. You should have told Max the truth. As for Durrant, he's a killer. If I were you, I'd watch out for that one."

"Santiago, I couldn't say much to Max. He's a fiend. I wish I could get away from him. I need help. I only went along with Durrant because I'm afraid of him, and Erich watches me all the time. I want to get to Venezuela. If I paid you well, would you help me, please, *querido*," Estelle fluttered her eyelids looking like a pathetic helpless child, which Thorne knew very well she was not.

"I'm not your *querido*," he said with disdain. "Why don't you just go to Galveston or one of the Texas ports, get on a boat? Why didn't you go to Vera Cruz when you were in Mexico?"

"Because it was too dangerous. I went to see my mother and sister but they had already gone. I couldn't do anything with Danson and Durrant always at my side. Durrant wanted me to go with him. When I saw you I felt sure you were the one to help me. I like you, Santiago, we are good together."

Thorne smiled, his back was itching. He wished she would go. "I can't help you, Estelle. Get one of your *vaqueros* to take you to Texas. He would cost far less than I would, if I were to take on the task," he said, looking coldly at her.

There was a knock at the door. Estelle looked alarmed. Thorne got up angrily. When he opened the door

Durrant stood there looking worried.

"Kugler's in town," he said pushing his way in. Estelle blanched, then Pat Crenna came swinging around the corner and when he saw Durrant, whipped out his Colt, levelling it at him.

"Shut the door," Thorne called to him, "and put the gun away, Deputy."

Crenna, taking Thorne's hint, closed the door. "Sorry, Mr Santiago, I didn't know . . . "

"It's all right. Nothing to worry about. I'll see you later," Thorne said evenly.

Giving Thorne a look, Crenna went out and went quickly to his room and put an ear to the wall.

"Who was that?" Estelle asked. "I've never seen him before. He's a deputy?" She shuddered.

Durrant shrugged, "Search me!" He'd taken a good look at Crenna and noticed the missing teeth. He also had noted that the man wore no star. He was probably Santiago's helper, he thought. "Come on, *señora*. Let's go while Kugler is in the store."

Estelle picked up her riding gloves and crop. "I hope you soon recover," she told Thorne. "Oh, by the way, are you really a federal agent?"

She'd said it so quickly Thorne almost said no. "Now you know I can't discuss that," he said giving her a brief smile. "Take care," he called after her as Durrant hustled her away.

Thorne sat down and lit a cheroot. A moment later Crenna came in. "They've gone," he said. "You OK?" he asked looking worriedly at Thorne who was sweating now. "What did the bitch want?"

"I might have found out if Durrant hadn't arrived, but I think it was to discover what I might be doing next. She offered me *mucho dinero* to take her away from Singer. Then she asked me if I was an agent."

Crenna laughed. "I wouldn't trust that one out of sight. Durrant sure looked worried though about that big fella."

"I guess Singer sent him and her. He's worried. Pat, go buy some writing paper, envelopes and a pen and ink. Only don't go in the store until they are all gone. I'm sorry that Durrant had to see you."

"I like that — deputy, indeed. I sure as hell would look good in the sheriff's office. Folks'd be paying to come take a look at me," said Crenna laughing ruefully.

"There's worse jobs. They could use a deputy here," Thorne told him. "This place will grow."

★ ★ ★

It was late afternoon when Sheriff Willard arrived at Beaver's rooming-house and asked to see a man by name of Santiago. Buck Beaver took him through to the rear where Thorne sat catching the late afternoon sun. Beaver had some worried thoughts about this

Santiago and his sidekick. They were as different as chalk from cheese. He wanted no trouble.

Willard took an old wicker chair and planted himself near Thorne after introducing himself. "I understand you have been in the wars," he said looking Thorne over with a shrewd eye.

"You could say that," Thorne answered, warily. "How can I help you, Sheriff?"

"Well, the stage line are quite worried about a young teamster, Sam Pickard, who drove a coach up here on a special hire-out. He never came back to Las Cruces. Nobody seems to know why, or where he might have gone to. I'm wondering if you could shed some light on that, as I believe you travelled in, or escorted the coach."

"At a guess, Sheriff, I'd say your coach driver is now six feet under near a certain hacienda not far away. As a matter of fact I've just written a letter to your office in Las Cruces about

161

the said subject," Thorne explained to Willard.

Willard looked keenly at Thorne. "That so! Then I'm glad I came. You'd better tell me about what you're intimating."

Thorne got up, wincing. "Let's go inside, Sheriff. I'm sure you could use some coffee." He called to Beaver to fetch coffee and cake, then led Willard into his room, where the sheriff got out a notebook and pencil. He listened without interruption to what Thorne had to tell him. "So, how did you know it was this Durrant who shot the lad?" Willard asked when Thorne had given him the gist of things.

"After they took me, I saw Durrant go back to look for the driver after I'd mentioned they ought to see where he was. He came back and said the driver had tried to shoot him. We all heard two shots. I certainly saw Durrant shoot Danson. They took both bodies to the hacienda."

"We got a case of murder here then,"

said Willard. "I'll need a couple of deputies to go and arrest Durrant. I take it you will press charges against both him and Singer? I've seen the big fella a couple of times. He sure is big an' strong."

"He surely is, like a bear. You'll need help with him. But I'll let it go with him for the moment. He's just a dogsbody for Singer. Though he really enjoys his work. I'm making enquiries about Singer through government sources. I think they might want to take a look at any papers he may have," said Thorne.

"I'll send a telegraph to Las Cruces for help. My deputies can come on the stage and rent horses from the livery — be here by tomorrow afternoon. I'll see if Beaver has a spare room. I could use some sleep," said Willard and took himself off.

Crenna came in then looking pale. "What's going on? Where'd the sheriff come from?" he asked.

"He's come from Las Cruces about

the coachman. The stage line is asking."

"You told him?"

"Not about you. I kept you out of it. If you want to testify against Durrant, it's up to you. It will mean a trip back to Las Cruces, which is a nuisance, but if it means putting that lot in jail I don't mind. They will have to look for the bodies first. Singer should get jail for complicity, I'm hoping, and for beating me up."

"What about the gorilla?"

"I think he will make a fight of it. I'm hoping so. If they take Singer away he'll have no one. Once they have Singer then I'll press charges about Kugler. He'll take some handling," Thorne said. "You'd better stay out of sight, Pat. You don't know what Durrant might do if he gets the chance. Do you want to ride on out?"

"Where would I go? 'Sides you need taking care of," Crenna said, grinning.

"Go get us a bottle of whiskey. We'll invite the sheriff to join us after supper.

I'll say you're staying and looking for work here."

"If the sheriff talks to Ned Carter he'll tell him I brung you in," Crenna said, looking worried. "Other folks know too. Father Brady for one."

"Then we'll tell the sheriff tonight it was you who found me as you were riding through," said Thorne.

★ ★ ★

When Estelle got back with Durrant, Singer was having tea. "Well, you found out anything?" he snapped.

"Santiago is at Beaver's place. Madge Jackson has been taking care of him and Father Brady," she said.

Singer looked sombre. "Anything else?"

"He might be an agent. I asked him. He said he couldn't discuss it."

"He's bluffing," Durrant interjected. "A gunrunner an agent. Never!"

"*Ja*, but it could be a good cover. America sells arms to other countries

165

like Cuba," said Singer.

"Erich was in town, boss. You got him following me?" Durrant changed the subject.

"I sent him to get stores. He's no good with the horses," was all Singer offered. "You better see the guards keep a good lookout. If any strangers come on my land, you give them a warning shot. Send them away."

"OK, boss," Durrant replied and went out. Kugler was coming through the outer gate. "One day, *amigo* . . . " Durrant muttered and went to put his horse away.

12

THORNE had slept deeply after drinking several shots of whiskey. Pat Crenna woke him around nine. "You want breakfast?" he enquired. "I'll bring it for you."

"You'd make a good valet," Thorne said laughing, after Pat had shaved him.

"You ever have one, Santi?" Crenna asked.

"You gotta be kidding," Thorne replied, alert to the fact that Pat was ferreting. He liked the aura of mystery he'd woven around himself. It gave him a sense of importance. What would Grandpa Hasler have thought of such notions, he wondered? "Never be ashamed of who you are, Rudi," he had once told him. "You live right, that is what counts." Thorne shuddered at what he would have said about the

167

gun-running exploits. His mind moved to thoughts of East Texas. It would be cold there soon. That was the place he was thinking of putting down roots.

"Hey, Santi!" Pat burst in on his cogitating. "Madge has a daughter. I just seen her and she's real prime. Big brown eyes and a sassy way with her!"

"Oh, is that so?" was all Thorne could muster as he got his mind back to the present. How was the sheriff filling in his day, he wondered?

Willard, in fact, was at the telegraph office. A reply had come back to his query to say that two deputies were *en route* by coach. Good, that would give him time before dark to pick up Durrant and Singer. Get them in for questioning. Singer must have ordered the bodies be taken and buried, so he was guilty of accessory to murder. There'd be others to question too. He got the key to the small lock-up jailhouse from the telegraph operator. He must press for it to be opened on a permanent basis and have a deputy installed. Hatch would be spreading out once the rail tracks ran down to El Paso. He went back to Beaver's and lay on his bed. Who was this man Santiago? Was he all that he seemed to be, he wondered? As for the other one, Crenna — well.

The stage rolled in on time and the two deputies, Vic Morrow and Ed Bradley went to the jailhouse then to the livery to hire two horses. Ned Carter's dad picked out two good mounts for them, and sent Ned to get Willard. Soon all three were on their way to the hacienda.

Thorne and Crenna watched them go apprehensively. "That's one chore I'd not wish to be taking on," said Pat.

"Nor me," Thorne replied. "Though with a legal warrant it's different. If they give you any trouble you can shoot them or lay them out and manacle them."

"Them three would never bring in

that gorilla," Pat said sagely.

"I know, that's why I didn't lay charges against him yet," Thorne replied.

"What if that bitch and Singer say you were lying and make out like you was in it with Durrant?" Pat asked.

"I think Estelle will say as little as possible, Singer too."

"I been thinking if that Singer gets sent to jail or something was to happen to him, she'd get the lot, hacienda, stock and whatever dough he's got," Pat said.

"I think when they dig up those two bodies and check the bullets in them, it won't look too good for any of them. I had no part in that, and I was a prisoner there and beaten. There's plenty of witnesses."

"Yeah, well I never thought of that — women!" Pat said, shaking his head.

Father Brady came up to them. "Did I see a lawman with deputies riding west?" he asked.

"Yes, Father," said Crenna. "They're

going for Singer and Durrant."

"Mother of God!" Brady said. "There'll be bloodshed for sure."

"You feel like a whiskey?" Thorne asked Brady.

"Come on, Father," Crenna urged the prevaricating priest. "It's good for your rheumatics."

Brady smiled. "Now it would at that," he said, and went inside with the two men who intrigued him considerably. Crenna he was beginning to like. Madge Jackson had told him, "There's a lot of good in Pat," and Madge was a good judge of men. About Santiago she'd held back her opinion.

★ ★ ★

Durrant was at the corral when he saw the three riders being let in through the outer gate. He supposed they were coming to look at horses. When he took a good look at their apparel, he walked hurriedly back to the main building and stood at the corner. Christ! They

171

were wearing stars. He backed up and almost ran to his room where he hurriedly dragged out a duffel bag and threw his spare clothes into it, and a few other items. Then he picked his mackinaw off a peg, took up his rifle, and a bedroll, and went out through the passageway and across to the barn where he saddled up his almost black gelding. When he led the horse out he saw Kugler coming. That bastard had eyes in the back of his head. He had his sawn-off shotgun in his hand. "Erich," Durrant called to him. "You'd best go help the boss, he's gonna need you. Them three lawmen, they've come for him I reckon. I'll go down the trail a piece, and when they head back, I'll blast 'em. You hear me?"

"Boss, he done nothing," Kugler shouted somewhat uncertainly. Durrant saw panic in Erich's eyes. Yes you bastard, without Singer you're a dead man. "That Santiago, he's laid charges against you and Singer. They'll be after you next. You look after yourself;

Singer won't help you."

As Durrant well knew, Kugler was a mite slow up in the belfry. His bluff worked and Kugler turned and went running back. "Jeez, he'll blast that posse to hell and then some," Durrant grinned.

Vic Morrow was on his way to the corral after a Mexican woman had told him where to find the men. He saw the big yellow-haired man running, and he saw the shotgun. Willard had warned him about Kugler. He sprang behind a huge terracotta plant pot and a second later the whole thing was blasted apart sending dirt and debris every which way. Morrow yelped as buckshot took him in the wrist. "Son'bitch," he cursed, and took off back into the inner yard and leapt over a bottom door of a loose box. Satan let out a scream and came at him teeth bared. Vic hit him on the nose with his rifle and the stallion backed away. "Sorry fella," said Morrow and ducked down below the door.

As Kugler ran into the yard, Bradley and Estelle were coming out and she was chatting and smiling up at the deputy. She saw Kugler, and for a moment was very scared. She put up a hand. "It's all right, Erich. The sheriff is talking with Max. Better not go in there now, he wouldn't like it."

Kugler just stood there, his eyes with a wild look in them, then he turned and walked away.

Durrant was at the gate about to open it and ride out. Bradley coming out through the arch called to him. "Mister, you'd better come on back. I've got to talk with all the staff here." From the corner of his mouth he said to Estelle, "Is that him?"

Estelle said, "yes," still smiling.

Morrow had now come out from the loose box and joined Bradley. Durrant cursed. He was considering making a run for it, but they could easily pick him off from where they stood. He came back riding easy.

"You going somewhere?" Morrow

asked taking note of the duffel bag and gear.

"Yes, up to Socorro to bring back two young horses for Mr Singer, isn't that so, *señora?*" Durrant gave Estelle a hard look.

Estelle said, "Max doesn't tell me all his business."

Morrow walked over, his six-gun in his hand. "You Jack Durrant?" he asked, watching Durrant keenly.

"Yeah, that's me! What do you want?" Durrant enquired rather hostilely.

"I've a warrant for your arrest for the murder of a Fred Danson, and possibly the coach driver who was hired to drive the *señora* up to Hatch from Las Cruces," said Morrow.

"Fred Danson? Who in hell told you that? Fred was shot by a fella called Santiago. Tell him, *señora.*" Durrant gave Estelle a pleading look.

"I didn't see who shot Fred, I was in the coach and knocked out when it turned over," Estelle said, not meeting Durrant's eyes.

Morrow fetched a pair of manacles from a pocket and swiftly put them on to Durrant's wrists, then tied his hands to the pommel.

Durrant was looking daggers at Estelle but still she did not look at him. She was afraid, as he'd seemed almost ready to spring at her before they put the manacles on him. Durrant was looking around in desperation for Kugler. Now he could use his help.

Morrow and Bradley spoke with the wranglers who'd been with Singer to meet the coach. Cooper, as main spokesman, gave his version of what had happened. None of them had seen who had shot Danson. Cooper said he thought that Santiago might have shot at Durrant, hitting him in the arm. Not one of them referred to what had happened to Sam Pickard.

Willard was feeling frustrated. It was Santiago's word against theirs. He would have to get the two bodies dug up to see what kind of slugs were in them, and Pickard's widow would want his body back for burial in Las Cruces. The sheriff was angry; Pickard was, had been, only twenty-four years of age. He still had to take Singer in for the brutal whipping. The big fella he would deal with tomorrow. It was coming dark and he wanted both Durrant and Singer locked up in the jail tonight. He spoke to Cooper. "You saddle up Mr Singer's horse; we'll be leaving in ten minutes. I'd not advise any attempt to stop us, or you'll be cut down if you do," Willard said evenly, his eyes cold hard, and Cooper knew the sheriff meant it.

Estelle sat with her husband as Willard told him his intention. Singer shrugged. "You're making a big mistake, Sheriff. Stell, I'll be back in the morning, you stay here," he told her meaningfully.

"Max," she whispered. "Erich, he'll do something. I'm afraid of him."

"I'll speak to him, he'll do as I say," Singer told her and went to put on his three-quarter-length wool coat. It looked as if it would rain and was turning cold.

Kugler stood in the hall, the shotgun cradled in his arms. "You not take my boss. He done nothing," he said menacingly.

"Erich," Singer spoke sharply. "Put the gun down. I'm going to help the sheriff. I'll be back in the morning. You stay here and look after things. Cooper will be in charge of other matters." He walked over to Kugler and spoke next to his ear. "You touch my wife, I'll kill you," he said so's no one else could hear, then he strode out of the house not even looking back at Estelle.

★ ★ ★

It was raining and quite dark when Willard and the deputies put Singer and Durrant into the iron-barred cell which had in it two wooden bunks with old damp mattresses, one pillow and a threadbare blanket each.

"We'll catch pneumonia in here,"

178

Singer protested.

"Get the stove going boys," Willard called out. "I'll see you get food and coffee," he told Singer.

"I want a bottle of whiskey — two, in fact. I have money, here." He handed it to Vic Morrow. "This place isn't fit to keep hogs in," he added angrily.

Durrant said nothing, he was figuring that the sheriff had no real evidence that he'd shot Danson. Singer might get a couple of months for whipping Santiago. But they'd have to let him go, then the first thing he would do was kill that bitch. She could have helped him. Then he'd get that Santiago before he left Hatch.

The deputies took it in turn to guard the two prisoners. They doubted anyone would attempt to break them out. There'd been a bad atmosphere at the hacienda. Tomorrow they would be talking with the *vaqueros* and the big fella. For him they'd need leg irons as well as manacles.

After Singer and Durrant had been taken away, Estelle slipped upstairs. Kugler had ensconced himself in the living-room and she'd not dared to throw him out. He had the shotgun and a knife with him. What Max had whispered to him, she didn't know. She put her little derringer into a pocket; it probably wouldn't kill Erich if he tried anything, but it might stop him. From a silver pillbox she took a small pill and put it with the gun and went downstairs again. There was a warmth in the room as Erich had stoked up a big fire within the large stone hearth.

"Go get your supper, Erich, then tell them to bring the coffee in here," she said commandingly.

Erich was about to refuse but his hunger got the better of him. He left without a word. One day, he told himself, he would fix that bitch. He was smiling as he thought about Durrant. He hoped they would hang him. He would go and watch that with real pleasure.

Estelle had hardly finished her meal before Erich came back. "Coffee's coming," he told her and planted himself in Singer's favourite chair.

"Don't sit there," Estelle said coldly. You ought not to be in here at all."

"Boss say I look after things," he retorted.

Estelle regarded him with loathing in her eyes. "He might not come back, then what will you do, Erich?" she said spitefully.

For a moment Kugler had a look of real panic on his face, then a hungry leer slid over it. "If he don't come back . . . "

Constantia Torres came in with the coffee and some fruit which she placed before Estelle who sat at the dining-table at the end of the big room. The girl took away her empty plate and left. Estelle busied herself pouring the coffee, thinking it was an outrageous waste letting Kugler use one of her best china cups. She slipped the small pill into his cup then went over and placed it on a small table next to the chair he'd moved to. She was puzzled as to why they had not taken him with Max and Jack Durrant. Why hadn't Santiago laid charges against Erich? Suddenly she hated Santiago. He had refused to help her. There was a loud thump, and Kugler slid to the floor. Estelle smiled thinly and went over and lifted an eyelid. Then she went out to the kitchen and told the girl to fetch Cooper and two wranglers. "Señor Kugler has passed out," she told the girl who stood there agape.

When Cooper came in with a *vaquero* and a wrangler, he looked surprised. "What happened?" he enquired.

"The pig just fell over. I guess he's been drinking. He insisted that Max told him to stay in here. Take him and put him on his bed," Estelle told them.

"Well, I never. I didn't think Erich drank much more than a beer or two," said Cooper.

"Who can say," said Estelle. "I want him out of here. He frightens me."

"Me, too," said the wrangler, as they managed to get the big solid mound of dead weight off the floor.

Estelle shut and locked the door firmly after they were gone. Then she went to the bureau and started to work on the lock with a steel knife.

13

AFTER Sheriff Willard had finished his late meal at Beaver's, he found Thorne in the small lounge drinking coffee. "Ah, Santiago," he hailed him. "Singer and Durrant are locked up in the jailhouse, if you can call it that."

"Was there any trouble?" Thorne asked anxiously.

"Vic Morrow, one of my deputies took some buckshot from the big feller, in the wrist. Mrs Jackson is seeing to it. I see your friend Crenna is over there, helping out."

"Yes, she gave him a bed and he's doing chores for her, chopping wood, replacing shingles and whatever," Thorne replied.

"I've been wondering about him. Morrow says he was in Las Cruces recently, disappeared about the same time the black coach left town."

Santiago said, "Hm!" and sipped at his coffee. "Care for a snort?" he asked Willard, and took the whiskey bottle off the floor next to him, then got up and found another glass. Whiskey, he had discovered was a more acceptable way of killing pain than laudanum.

"If you insist," said Willard, thinking that this Santiago was a smooth cuss.

"I've decided to press charges against Kugler," said Thorne. "I didn't think you could manage him with the other two."

Willard gave a tired smile. "I might have to let Durrant go. Those wranglers who were with Singer said they never saw Durrant shoot at either Danson or the driver."

"Well, before Singer came along, Durrant had hold of some bags he had thrown out of the coach. It was quite obvious to me he meant to ride off with them. I'm not sure if the *señora* intended going with him, but I didn't know then that she had been knocked out. She had already told me she was afraid of Durrant when she asked me to help her, in Las Cruces. I think she tried to poison Durrant, as he passed out after he'd drunk some coffee. The doctor said he thought it was food poisoning. So, why did all three of them not have it, I asked myself? She obviously used me and Durrant, who is a killer. I saw him shoot Danson. I'd say she married Singer to get her out of Mexico. She said her father and brother were killed, her mother and her sister had fled into hiding. She came yesterday and offered me money to help her get away. I refused. She is trying to get to Venezuela to join her mother. She'll try anything to get help now, I think."

"I see. Well I'm not interested in her. Are you a gun-runner, Santiago? A good lawyer could rip you apart in court, if Singer takes you on," Willard said, giving Santiago a keen look.

"I sold guns, yes. Guns the army no longer needed. That fiend whipped me for no good reason. If someone hadn't fired shots and distracted him, I believe he would have killed me. You should speak to the old Mexican, Timo, probably part Indian. He was kind to me. I think he knows plenty about Singer.

"The army doesn't particularly like it known that they sell old surplus guns to anyone who will buy them. They have cut down their forces drastically and have issued repeater carbines now. Peter Varig lives down in Mexico and buys arms and ammunition. I saw a lot I did not like this time, while down there, so I'm through with it. Yes, I made some money. I killed a few Apaches and one or two bandits. If I'm guilty of something, you tell me what, Sheriff," Thorne said, and took another long swallow of whiskey.

"I guess I can get Durrant for killing Danson then; Singer and Kugler for beating you up. We're digging up the two bodies tomorrow and we'll take a look at the slugs in 'em. I have

Durrant's side-gun. He was about to take off; we just got him in time, so that says something about him. They'll have to be taken to Las Cruces, we have a judge there. It would be best if your friend Crenna came with you to say how he found you and what state you were in," Willard told Santiago, knocking out his pipe against the fire grate.

"I don't know if he will come. He's an army deserter. I'd prefer you keep him out of it. He ran away because of the bullying sergeant who used a whip on him more than once. He's a decent man just down on his luck. I used him once to go into Mexico. If you could protect him, perhaps." Thorne looked at Willard, poured him another drink.

"Might be," said Willard. "Anyway, the army is not my concern. Hell, this is a difficult one. I'd prefer a straightforward bank robbery, you know where you're at. I ain't no detective."

"I think you'll handle it right enough, Sheriff," Thorne said. "I wouldn't be surprised if you were to find more than two bodies out there."

Willard finished his drink. "I'm for bed. I gotta get up early," he told Thorne and left the room.

In the morning Willard left Vic Morrow in charge of the jail, and after swearing in two volunteers, good hefty men presently out of work and glad of the two bucks and meals, he rode out with them and Ed Bradley just before 8 a.m. A Mexican guard let them in through the outer gate and they went straight to the corral where Vince Cooper waited with four wranglers and several vaqueros. "Good morning, Sheriff," he said somewhat coolly. "I see you haven't brought the boss back with you."

"No, he'll not be back for some time. We'll be taking him down to Las Cruces to the court there. I guess you'd best look after things if you're the foreman," Willard said sharply. "First I want those bodies dug up. Pick some men, and let's get on with it." Willard looked up at the sky hoping it would not start to rain.

Willard and the others followed Cooper who had told two Mexican peons who worked around the buildings and the gardens to start digging where they had buried the bodies under a stand of trees some way out from the gate across the trail. Bradley and Willard smoked stogeys as they waited. When the bodies were finally lifted out, Willard swore. How was he going to tell Pickard's wife? They'd only been married lately. "Get a wagon and put them into it," he snapped.

"You get the bastard who shot Fred Danson," a wrangler called out angrily. "Santiago!"

"Did you see who did it?" Bradley swung round. "Did anyone?"

There was a silence. Everyone shuffled uneasily. "There's no Doc in town," Bradley said to Willard.

"Madge Jackson can do it, I guess, unless you want to, Ed," Willard said pointedly.

Bradley turned away and threw up his breakfast. Willard suddenly pointed a finger at a peon who was looking scared. "You, are there any more bodies on this hacienda? You dig more graves?" His eyes swept round the men who stood there. No one said a word. Then, just as they were going back in through the gate, Pedro Lopez spotted Erich Kugler coming out through the arch. He muttered something under his breath. Willard gave him a look, then saw Kugler. He turned to Cooper. "Where's the one called Timo?"

"He works in the yard, does the loose boxes and sweeps up. He keeps to himself mostly," said Cooper.

Kugler stood waiting for them. Willard noted he still carried the shotgun, and there was a large knife hanging in a scabbard at his belt. He suddenly made up his mind and walked swiftly around the big one and hit him hard over the head with his long barrelled Colt. Kugler who was looking red-eyed dropped forward on to his knees, a surprised look on his face before he passed out and fell forward on his face. "Get those leg irons and manacles on him quick," Willard told his possemen. "I guess that will save a lot of trouble."

Cooper said. "Jeezus Christ!" All the *vaqueros* crossed themselves hurriedly, and grinned. "What was that for, Sheriff?"

"To save time and bloodshed. He's wanted for the brutal beating of one, Santiago. I've got no time to struggle with him. Put him in the wagon, boys, after you cover the bodies with tarpaulin."

One of the wranglers said, "Well, I'll be damned! Somebody actually floored big Erich. I sure hope you got a strong jail cell, Sheriff."

Estelle had seen Kugler walking across the yard with his gun. At least she'd had a peaceful night. She had managed to open the bureau and found a lot of greenback dollars stashed in a box which she had opened with one of her own keys. There were some documents she didn't understand, and one signed by the previous owner, Stanton. She did not care about the hacienda. It was a lonely place. Neither did she care what happened to Max. She knew now for sure he had betrayed her father and brother. This morning she had spoken with Emelio Alvarez and he had said he would take her to Galveston. They could take two horses each so they could sell them before they took passage on a ship to Venezuela. That he was willing to go all the way there with her surprised her. But on thinking it over she saw it would be most sensible, he could protect her from the gringos who liked to put their hands on a woman travelling alone, not to mention others who might well be at the towns they must ride through. It would be a long hazardous journey, but to stay here waiting for Max to return, she simply could not contemplate. She put a welcoming smile on her face as

Willard came into the courtyard. "Good morning, Sheriff. I see you have not brought my husband with you!"

"Unfortunately, no, *señora*. Santiago will not retract his charges, so your husband will have to go to Las Cruces for trial, and Jack Durrant also, and now the big one, he too, now charges have been laid against him. We have him in the wagon, with the two bodies. I wonder if you have remembered anything more about the incident when the coach turned over?"

Estelle frowned. "I did hear one of the wranglers, I can't say which one, say that Jack Durrant had shot the driver, because he tried to kill him."

"You'd testify to that?" Willard asked.

"No, I did not see him do it. So, that is only hearsay. You must ask the men," Estelle said. "But I wouldn't be surprised if Durrant did shoot Fred. I was unconscious, as you know."

Willard gave a brief smile. She's one smart lady, he was thinking. "I'd like to speak to your man, Timo. Is he around?" he asked her.

Estelle looked surprised. "He should be, he cleans the yard and looks after the stables, and *el Diablo*," she said shuddering.

"*Señor*," a soft voice spoke behind Willard. He swung round. "You look for me?"

"Yes, I'd like to ask you some questions," said Willard looking closely at the old man. He decided he was probably half-Indian, as Santiago had said.

"You can use the tack-room," Estelle told Willard. "I'll have some coffee sent out." She smiled sweetly.

Bradley came into the yard. "It's going to rain, Vern. Shall I send the wagon off?"

"Yes, and you go with it and Brimble. Leave Scott, I might need him. If that big bastard starts anything, hit him again," Willard said frustratedly.

Sipping the good coffee appreciatively, Willard regarded the old man who sat opposite in an old hide-bound chair. His face was like a walnut shell. It would be hard to guess at his age. There was a softness in the eyes and intelligence, he could see. "Tell me, Timo, how long have you been at the hacienda?"

"*Siete años, señor.*"

"So you worked for George Stanton, then?"

"*Si, señor.* He *bueno hombre.*"

"You must have been sorry when he sold up and went away. A sick man, I heard."

"No. Señor Stanton not go, he *muerto.*"

Willard's eyes slitted. He suddenly felt little beads of sweat on his brow and took out a handkerchief and wiped it. "Stanton did not leave? He's *muerto*, dead? I don't understand," Willard said somewhat shaken.

Timo took the cigar Willard offered him and sat a moment, drawing in the smoke, then expelling it. "The *bastardo gringo, el grande toro.* He *exterminer!*"

Willard leaned forward. "Erich Kugler, he killed Señor Stanton?"

"*Si*, he take on wagon with valise. Go Hatch. Me out look for *ciervo*. The wagon stop. Kugler pull the *cuchillo* so." Timo drew his fingers across his throat. "Gringo take wagon off track, put Stanton in back, then drink *mucho* whiskey, sleep, then is dark go hacienda."

"Mother of God! What are you telling me, Timo?" Willard was sweating now. "You say Kugler was taking Stanton to Hatch, but he stopped on the trail, slit his throat, then covered him up in the wagon and waited until it got dark, giving himself plenty of time to have gone to Hatch and back. So, what happened to Stanton's body?"

Timo got up. "Come I show," he walked off on his moccasined feet. Willard followed feeling the hair on his neck stand up. He sure as hell would not have liked to come up against Timo when he was young. Not even now. He spoke Mexican and some English but he figured the old man had once spoken the Apache lingo. Must have had a Mex father and an Indian mother.

Timo stopped at the loose box where the black stallion was poking its head over the lower door. He said something to the horse they called Satan. The horse nickered. Willard stood waiting. "Señor Stanton," Timo said, and pointed at the floor of the loose box.

Willard looking puzzled watched Timo, awestruck, as the old man clipped a lead rope to the horse's collar led him out and tied him to a ring in the wall, a few feet away. The old man then went inside and scruffed the straw with his feet and pointed. "Señor Stanton *aqui*."

Willard stood stupefied for some moments staring at the floor. It was hard pack. Three years Stanton must have been down there. Oh God! What a place, no one would ever suspect. No one but Timo, apparently dared go in there to bring the beast out. He moved and went in a hurry to fetch Bert Scott, who was talking with the *vaqueros* in the barn. "Bring spades," he shouted at them, "and hurry," he said grimly.

Estelle, who was getting impatient, came out to the yard to see what the commotion was about as Willard, followed by Scott was crowding around the loose box which the stallion usually occupied, only now he was tied at the wall and snorting and moving about. Timo came over to quieten him. Estelle skirted around the horse of which she was terrified and went to see what they were at. She spoke to Willard in agitated fashion. "What is going on?"

"We'll find out soon," was all he told her. He got another cigar going and puffed at it furiously.

Cooper and a *vaquero* were digging hurriedly, someone had brought a pick. After almost half an hour, when about four feet down, they found a skull. Looking sick, Cooper came out for air.

"Oh man, who is that down there?" he asked Willard.

"George Stanton, the previous owner, I believe," said Willard, also looking sick.

"Oh no!" Estelle shrieked, going quite pale. "Who put him down there? When? Under that devil horse!" She looked aghast at Willard. He was convinced she'd had no idea, had nothing to do with it.

"According to Timo, your good man had him killed by that big gorilla, Erich Kugler," Willard said tersely.

"I don't understand. Max said he went back East. He was a sick man, that's why he had to sell up." She looked strickenly at Willard.

"He was sick all right. A knife across his throat according to Timo," said Willard caustically. "You got it all, boys?" he asked, as the *vaquero* came out with bones and some rotted clothing.

"I know nothing of this, Sheriff," Estelle told Willard. She was plenty scared now. "Max was a cruel man. I was going to leave him only I was scared he would send that pig Erich after me."

"All right, Señora Singer, I believe you. Only you'll probably be called to testify at the trial. This is a murder case now. Anyway you don't need to be afraid. They will all be taken to Las Cruces tomorrow. You'd best get in out of the rain," Willard said as the rain spots hit his face.

14

WHEN Sheriff Willard got back to Hatch he was relieved to find that Kugler had been safely transported there. He knew what a man of his size and strength could be capable of if he went beserk. Madge Jackson had already removed the bullet from Danson's back and two from young Pickard's chest. "I'm sorry you had to do such a chore," he told Madge. "There was no one else who would do it, and I needed to see the slugs quickly."

"It's all right, Sheriff. My late husband was a doctor and he taught me a lot about such things. I often helped him when he removed bullets, though it was usually from live men. There is one thing, though: Sam Pickard did not die from those bullets, he was already dead from a broken neck, there was no bleeding."

"Damn!" said Willard. "Then I can't charge that bastard Durrant with murder. Though there's no one but Santiago saying that Durrant did shoot him, and it is only from what he heard a wrangler repeat that Durrant had said he'd had to shoot because Pickard had fired at him."

"That monster, he must have shot at him in cold blood since he was already laid there dead," Madge said angrily. "Then charge him with intent."

"I think once I talk with that yellow-haired son of a . . . sorry Madge, he'll probably tell me the truth. I think he don't like Durrant much. He'll stick up for Singer, but I've got them both for Stanton's murder. An old Mex saw it all and he showed us where they'd buried him, and I got his mark on a statement. I reckon Singer told Kugler to put the body beneath that devil stallion in his loose box. It nearly got Vic Morrow, came right at him when he went in there."

"Just to think, poor George was down there all this time. Father Brady was quite put out when he never came to say goodbye. They used to play chess together, and were real good friends," Madge said sadly, wiping her nose vigorously.

"Well he can have a decent burial now. We know it was him as Timo and a *vaquero* recognized his jacket — what was left of it. No one who had worked for Stanton would have ever thought he might be killed like that. Timo said nothing, he was probably afraid of Singer and he needed a job. Being part Indian, I guess he kept his thoughts to himself, especially about us white folks. Anyway Kugler will hang and Singer will get a nice long term in the penitentiary, I hope," said Willard, taking out his pipe and tobacco.

"Amen to that!" said Madge. "D'you think Estelle Singer knew about it?"

"I doubt it. It would be done before she arrived there. I understand she was in El Paso some time before Singer brought her up there."

"Why kill George?" Madge wondered. "It doesn't make sense to me."

"My guess is that Singer hadn't a lot of dough. He fled out of Mexico, I believe. So he killed Stanton after paying him in cash and took the money back before George could get to a bank. That's where the big fella came in. He seems to be dedicated to Singer. Singer would then send the records to the land office which Stanton would have signed over to him after the sale. If Singer has no citizenship papers he had a reason to lay low out at the hacienda. Who comes out here looking into things? If the *señora* hadn't gone to Mexico on that trip and got mixed up with Santiago, whatever, none of this would have happened and poor old George's remains would have stayed down in that loose box till Kingdom come, I should think. Singer probably knew that Stanton was a widower and had no offspring, and probably no relatives. He was a close-mouthed feller was Stanton, so I've been told. Anyrate, that's what I think," said Willard, blowing a cloud of smoke from his mouth.

"That makes sense to me," Madge concurred. "I wonder what will happen to Estelle?"

"Oh, I think she'll sell up and *vamanos*. She'll probably go find her mother and sister wherever they may be. I think she'll be capable of looking after herself, that one," said Willard sagely.

★ ★ ★

When Bradley went to the jailhouse to see the prisoners, Durrant protested loudly. "I'm not staying in here with him." He nodded towards Kugler.

"You ain't got no say in the matter, Durrant. Tomorrow you'll be transferred to Las Cruces to await your trial," Bradley told him.

"You'll never get us there," said Durrant in a taunting fashion. He was extremely worried though.

206

When Willard came and formally charged Kugler with George Stanton's murder, and Singer with instigating it, there was a deadly silence for some moments until Singer said, quite unconcernedly, "I know nothing about it. I paid Stanton for the land, stock and all buildings. Erich took him to Hatch. We never saw or heard from him again. I think it is possible that the body you found was someone else. Someone put there before I came to the hacienda. You have no reason to hold either Kugler or myself. You are holding us under false pretences."

"We have a witness who saw Kugler kill Stanton and the both of you carry the body later after dark. Then you buried him in that box and put the stallion in there so no one would go nosing about. You made a big mistake there, Singer," said Willard, suddenly not so sure of himself. What if it wasn't Stanton?

Singer looked momentarily shaken.

"Witness, what witness? How can this be so?"

"Your yardman, Timo. He saw Kugler kill Stanton out along the trail, then he brought him back after dark to show you what a good boy he'd been. Jest like a cat bringing a mouse. He saw you both bury Stanton; we got his mark on a statement."

Singer was red in the face. Durrant had sat up and was lapping up Willard's discourse with gleeful interest. "That old man," Singer expostulated, "he drinks pulque, he hallucinates, he'll say anything for a buck or two. How much you pay him, Sheriff?"

"He sure as hell wasn't hallucinating about where you put Stanton. Both he and a *vaquero* who worked for Stanton have identified Stanton's jacket. You'll hang, both of you," Willard said, and left in a hurry before he lost his rag good and proper.

"Jeezus!" said Durrant. "Nobody would go in that box except Timo. How much did you pay him, Singer?"

"You shut up!" Kugler said, sitting up. So far he'd kept quiet. He knew he and Singer were in real trouble. He still had a bad headache from the pill Estelle had given him and the rap over the head. It was difficult for him to concentrate on anything at the moment as he lay on a mattress between the two bunks, his legs in irons.

Durrant was busy thinking how he could get away tomorrow. He had been charged with intent to kill. He was feeling extremely worried now. Somehow he must get them to discharge Santiago's testimony. If only Estelle would say something against that bastard.

★ ★ ★

When young Ned Carter arrived quite early at the hacienda he was met by Vince Cooper who came into the courtyard. "I got a letter here for Mrs Singer," he told him. "An' I got one for you from Singer. They're taking all three of them varmints down to Las Cruces today. So you better be quick if you or the *señora* want to go see them."

Cooper took the envelopes and tore open one which was addressed to him. "Ned, go to the kitchen and get some coffee or something before you go back," he told the lad, who took up the offer with alacrity. With luck, he might have a few words with Constantia Torres.

Singer's note told Vince that he should take care of things until he came back. Well, that might be some time, Cooper thought. Maybe never. What the hell would the señora do about it all, he wondered, as he took her envelope inside. Things were sure as hell in a mess.

He found Estelle in the living-room. The bureau, he could see had been ransacked. So, she'd started already to help herself. He handed her the note and she snatched it eagerly. He could not tell from her expression what it contained. "It's all right, Vince, Max says you're to look after things until he comes back."

"You think he'll be back, *señora*? It don't look good for him. You ought to think on things. If I can help . . . "

"Thank you, Vince. I'll call on you if . . . Just do what you normally do. It might be a good idea if you know of anyone interested in buying this place — just in case. It's all been such a shock. I really don't want to stay here, it gives me the shivers."

"Yeah, that it do," said Cooper, and went on his way to give orders to the men. If only he had some real dough, he could buy the place himself. One thing though, he was thinking, there sure was a better atmosphere this morning without that damned big son'bitch Kugler around. Even Timo had been smiling briefly.

★ ★ ★

Willard had telegraphed for two extra men to meet him at an old fort near some springs. Kugler, he feared could be a problem. He was looking much sharper this morning. By nine o'clock, the black coach with its wheel repaired was loaded up. Morrow and Bradley were inside with Kugler and Singer. Durrant was up top and manacled to an iron rail, his legs also had irons on them. Kugler was also manacled and wore leg irons. Singer was just manacled. He, according to Willard, was not likely to make a break for it. He was firmly convinced that he would walk free from the court. He had already had a telegraph sent to a lawyer he knew in Las Cruces. Willard rode shotgun with a muleskinner driving the four-horse team. He had no fears that any of Singer's men might try to rescue him. Nobody at the hacienda, he was sure, felt any such loyalty to him. Kugler was his main worry, and Durrant might try something; he had a look of desperation about him today.

The coach rolled out and went on its way in bright sunshine.

Crenna and Thorne watched the coach depart from a distance. "I'm sure glad they're gone," said Pat. "I won't feel happy though until they're on their way to the Territorial Prison. Heaven help the wardens who get to look after that gorilla."

Thorne said little. He was so quiet that Crenna glanced sideways at him. "It's a shame we gotta go back all that way to Las Cruces. You could've been on your way to wherever you was going by now," he said.

"I'm in no real hurry. Another week and I'll be in better shape to travel. We'll take the stage to Las Cruces, we have to take Timo with us, remember? Now you have decided to testify, it should all go quicker," Thorne answered.

"I hope so. I hope they don't ask me too much about my past. You think they will?" Pat said worriedly.

"There's no reason they should,

you're not on trial. Singer and the other two are. They might try to pull me apart. Make me seem like an unreliable witness. But there are three dead bodies to explain. They will concentrate on Stanton's murder mostly. I want those two hanged or put away for life. If Durrant gets off I'm not too worried, though he should hang for killing Danson who did nothing wrong, nor the lad," Thorne said bitterly.

★ ★ ★

At the way-station the three prisoners were taken one by one to relieve themselves. They were given coffee and a sandwich each. The two deputies had met up with the coach at the old fort, and were now riding just behind the coach, or when it was wide enough, would come abreast to check on things.

It was about two miles on from the way-station that Kugler decided to make his move. He was feigning sleep then suddenly he lifted his feet and struck out at Vic Morrow's legs. Morrow yelled and Bradley lifted up his rifle, but Kugler sprang at him sweeping his manacled wrists back and forth in their faces and both men were blinded, blood running from a cut above Morrow's eye. Singer, sitting close to the left-hand door, booted it open, and Kugler leapt out. He went head over heels down a bank.

Durrant, who had been working on a loose screw in the rail he was attached to, seized his opportunity as Willard leaned over to shout down to Bradley, "What the hell is going on?" The rail came loose and Durrant literally sprang down several feet landing in some bushes. Cursing as his legs banged on a stone, he scrambled in under the bushes. There was about two feet of chain between the irons, he could hardly run but it was his only chance now to get away. He got up and began to edge his way along through some young pine, hoping that Kugler would keep them all busy for a while. Perhaps if he could get to the muleskinner and get his rifle . . .

Don Taylor, one of the deputies who'd come from Las Cruces ran his horse down the slope after Kugler. He drew his side-arm as he approached the big yellow-haired hefty man who was hopping along like a dancing bear. "Hey, you! Stand still or I'll drop you," Taylor shouted. Suddenly Kugler turned and came roaring like a bull and was almost at the horse which took fright and pivoted round and round.

Stan Brunton, the other deputy, fired a shot down the slope at Kugler, and Willard who'd got down came running, almost going headlong over a tree stump also fired with his Colt. Kugler had turned and was now trying to run at Willard. Another rifle shot hit Kugler in the chest, but still he came on. Willard had himself under control now. He stood quite still and took aim. His bullet went into Kugler just between the eyes as he was roaring like a lion. For a moment he stood there shaking his head, then he fell on his back, hitting the ground so hard it shook.

Brunton got down off his horse and went over slowly. He peered down at Kugler.

"Is he dead?" called Taylor who now had his horse under control.

"Yep, I reckon so. He come on like a bear; I never seen the like, by God," said Brunton.

Willard was shaking. If he hadn't stopped Kugler the bastard would have got a bear hug on him and likely would have killed him, he was thinking.

It took four of them to drag Kugler back up the slope and get him on top of the coach, and rope him down. Durrant had been rounded up by Bradley and was now sitting in the coach looking like a trapped cougar. Singer was sitting smirking. There was no way they could get anything out of a dead corpse. Erich had killed Stanton and he could deny any knowledge of ordering him to do so. He could say the old man Timo had been mistaken about him helping bury Stanton.

Morrow who'd been vomiting after Kugler had hit him over the throat, was now riding shotgun. Willard sat inside with Bradley. He lit a stogey as they got underway again. He felt quietly confident he would have no more trouble now. Soon they'd be into Las Cruces.

15

THORNE and Crenna came out of the courtroom feeling relieved. A twelve-man jury had taken most of the day to arrive at their verdicts. They had taken Thorne's testimony first, listening intently. Everyone had gasped when he had been called upon to expose his back and show the weals from the beating. Crenna had given his version of how Thorne had asked him to accompany him to Hatch as Señora Singer had been afraid that two men, who she thought were Mexican Federales, were intent on doing her harm. Also she was not sure about Durrant. Neither he nor Thorne had seen any sign of these men, but they had witnessed Durrant's shooting of Fred Danson, and Crenna had seen Durrant shoot a man, the coach driver, while he was lying on the ground and not moving.

Singer had explained Señora Singer's absence, in that she was indisposed and could add nothing since she had been knocked out cold, and only recovered on the way to the hacienda. The lawyer had tried to destroy Thorne's evidence, saying he was a gun-runner and his reputation in question. Thorne had produced a bill of sale for the guns from an army ordnance colonel, and affirmed that he had done nothing illegal. The army was disposing of its old carbines and had a large surplus to get rid of as its forces had been run down. The judge said that the issue had little relevance to the case and dismissed the lawyer's accusations. He told the jury that the brutal whipping, and further beating by the now dead man, Kugler, had been contemptible.

As for the murder of George Stanton, after Timo had been called, his testimony read out in Spanish and English, and he had again affirmed that it was the truth, there was a late recess for luncheon.

Thorne took Crenna and the old man to a cantina, where he felt Timo would be more comfortable. He slipped him fifty dollars. "Because you were so kind to me — you brought me *agua*, and you have helped to bring justice. Well I hope so. I hope Singer and Durrant will get life sentences," he said bitterly.

By late afternoon it was over. Durrant was to be hanged, and Singer was to be taken to the Territorial Penitentiary to serve twenty-five years hard labour. Durrant had looked shattered, and slumped back into his chair. Singer's face blanched. He wiped sweat off his face and gave an accusing hard look at his lawyer.

In the evening Thorne and Crenna met Willard and Bradley in the Greasewood Saloon. "Have you seen Timo anywhere?" he asked the lawmen. "He disappeared when it was over."

"He'll probably have gone to the cantina to get stoned," said Crenna, laughing.

Bradley gave him a look. "He don't drink. Cooper told me. Well, just a beer or two and a cigar. I think he will be going down near the border. He might pick up some work there at a livery. He told me he had not long to go," he said.

Just then some blue-coats came in and sat at a table, making Crenna nervous. Two were lieutenants and one a sergeant. Bradley said, "There's been some Indian trouble. That's probably why Timo took off so fast. He told me he don't like blue-bellies."

Lieutenant Hennessy was fetching more drinks when he saw Thorne. Today he had been in court to watch. Only recently he had decided to quit the army and go to study law. When they had called Rudi Thorne, he had been astounded. He'd tried to guess his age. Thorne had looked drawn and pale. Hennessy, like everyone else, had gasped when Thorne had bared his back to show the weals. All morning he had wanted to go and speak to him, but there'd been no chance and then he'd been called back to duty. Another officer came in then and slapped Hennessy on the back. "Hennessy, old buddy, one more beer," he said grinning.

Thorne went rigid in his chair. His hand shook as he set his glass down, causing Crenna to say, "You all right? You look kinda pale, Santi?" Then he went red. "I guess I'll never get used to calling you by your real name. I just knew Santiago wasn't it, but you sure got the women all excited with all that mystery."

Thorne gave a brief smile. "It served its purpose," he said gruffly.

"You must have made a lot of dough?" said Bradley.

"Not so much as some," Thorne replied, and got up. "I'll go and get a bottle of whiskey," he said, and strode to the bar.

"Bit tetchy about them guns, ain't he?" said Bradley.

"I gotta be going, my wife will be

expecting me," Willard said.

"Me too," said Bradley. "You'll be leaving tomorrow then?" He looked at Thorne.

"Yes, there's no reason for me to stay," Thorne responded. "Pat, too, we left our horses at Hatch." They all shook hands and Thorne sat down again and poured two stiff drinks. He was feeling tired, it had been a long day. He was wondering if Hennessy was the right age. Hell, there must be plenty of Hennessys.

Hennessy, having enhanced his courage with two beers and a whiskey, got up and came over to Thorne's table. "May I?" he asked, dragging out a chair. Crenna went quite white.

"Surely," said Thorne, his stomach contracting.

"I saw you in court today. I'm thinking of leaving the army and taking up law. It's pretty boring out here. Say, did the army really sell off all those weapons?"

"Sure, they don't need 'em any

more, especially the old ones now they've got repeaters. No sense in letting them rust in a warehouse. Have a whiskey," Thorne said. "Pat, fetch another glass, will you?"

Hennessy leaned forward. "Rudi Thorne, I've been wondering, are you German?"

"No, half-English, half-German. My grandparents were German. You'll be related to a Charles Hennessy, perhaps?" Thorne asked, gripping his glass.

Crenna came back with a glass and poured it full of whiskey and handed it to Hennessy. The lieutenant took a sip. "He is my father. Your mother, what was her first name?" Hennessy asked, his eyes fixed on Thorne who was looking strained. Every bone in his body was aching, his heart was thumping.

"My mother, as I recall, was called Renata. My grandparents, Hasler."

"Oh, well! Little Rudi! By all that's — you must be my long

lost half-brother then," Jim Hennessy spluttered out.

Crenna who was listening intently, spluttered into his beer. "Holy Toledo! This sure is a hell of a day! All your secrets are coming out, Santi," he said, flushed profusely, and lifted his glass.

Thorne gave him a look. "Pat, I think you'd better go to bed, we have an early start tomorrow," he said looking sternly at him. Crenna took the hint and got up and left, though he would have loved to stay in spite of the blue-bellies.

"Little Rudi, Jesus!" Thorne gave a harsh laugh.

"Mama used to call you that, well, not lately," Hennessy said, looking rueful. "She did try to find you after she and father went back to Washington about six years ago, I think. My father once came to get you but your grandfather wouldn't let you go. He said he'd adopted you, and that was that."

Thorne felt shaken. He knew his grandfather had been angry that his only child had chosen to go hundreds of miles away, but he had always felt his mother could have taken him. He would have been torn, that he knew now. He had loved his grandparents who'd given him a good life. "Well, I guess it's water under the bridge now," said Thorne. "It wasn't your fault."

"Hennessy, you coming?" one of his fellow officers called. "We got an early call."

"Listen," Hennessy said hurriedly, and pulled a piece of paper and a stub of pencil from a pocket. "I'll give you Mama's address. Father is pushing a desk in Washington now, he's a colonel. My sister Jane is married and lives in Richmond. She's having a baby soon, so we'll be uncles, I guess, then. Please write to Mama. She was ill for some time. She always worried about you. We lived so far away, Wyoming, Colorado, Arizona, it was a hard life for her. She loved father, still does. Your Pa, well, he drank, so I believe. I don't know what your plans are, but it would be splendid if we could all get together for Christmas, in Washington. I'll write and tell Mama I've seen you, that you're well. I won't tell her about Singer," Hennessy said pleadingly and gave Thorne the piece of paper with his parents' address on it. "I have to go now." He got up and Thorne too, they shook hands.

"Good luck to you," Thorne said. "Take care."

"You too. I'm surely glad I came into that courtroom today," Hennessy said smiling.

After he had gone, Thorne sat down and poured a large drink. He swallowed it, then got up and taking the bottle left the saloon. When he got outside he was feeling sick, shaking. Pull yourself together, Santi, he told himself. He blew his nose furiously and went to the hotel and up to his room. It sure as hell had been a long day. He suddenly felt very lonely.

★ ★ ★

It was about eight o'clock when Pat Crenna shook Thorne awake. "Hey, you figuring on making the stage at ten?"

Thorne sat up, his head throbbed and his mouth felt like the bottom of a birdcage. "Pat, go get a pot of black coffee. Better get two tickets on the stage first or we might not get on it," he said, scrambling up.

"I already got the tickets. All them blue-coats in town, I ain't hanging round here," said Crenna.

★ ★ ★

They were at the staging office when Willard came up to them, out of breath. "I'm glad I caught you. I've got some news. Singer is dead. He took poison. He must have had it on him. They found him in his cell this morning. I guess it'll save the taxpayers some dough. He'd never have survived the hard labour."

"I'm not surprised," said Thorne

soberly. "Now the *señora* will get it all, by God!"

"Yep, there was a will and the lawyer is taking the stage today. It'd be best you don't talk with him. But he'll be happy enough; he'll make plenty from the lady if he handles the sale, and I feel sure she'll be selling up, and taking off someplace," Willard replied.

"Well, at least she'll have plenty of funds to get her to Venezuela. She'll find someone fool enough to escort her, I'm sure. Too bad, Durrant played his cards so bad," Thorne said regretfully. Well, he had other plans now. It had occurred to him that Virginia was a whole lot prettier than East Texas. The colours were, as he recalled, magnificent in autumn and spring. It was a lot closer to Washington, too.

Crenna was grinning. "Now, if I hadn't lost my two front teeth, I might have offered my services to the *señora*. Hey, Santi why don't you go see her? She sure took a real fancy to you. You said you was looking for land. It'd be a real good partnership, an' I could be your top wrangler."

Thorne turned to Willard, ignoring Crenna. "I'm glad you came to tell us the news." They shook hands and Willard watched as Thorne turned to Crenna. "Why the hell don't you get into the stage-coach? I've got plans for you and they don't include the *señora*. We've got a lot of miles to cover. That's if you play your cards right." He gave Crenna a push, and turned and winked at Willard.

A few moments later the coach pulled out. Willard watched it as it hit the trail. Sure as hell are a danged strange pair, them two, he thought. Then he walked on back up the street. Tomorrow there was to be a hanging.

THE END

Other titles in the Linford Western Library:

TOP HAND
Wade Everett

The Broken T was big. But no ranch is big enough to let a man hide from himself.

GUN WOLVES OF LOBO BASIN
Lee Floren

The Feud was a blood debt. When Smoke Talbot found the outlaws who gunned down his folks he aimed to nail their hide to the barn door.

SHOTGUN SHARKEY
Marshall Grover

The westbound coach carrying the indomitable Larry and Stretch headed for a shooting showdown.

FIGHTING RAMROD
Charles N. Heckelmann

Most men would have cut their losses, but Frazer counted the bullets in his guns and said he'd soak the range in blood before he'd give up another inch of what was his.

LONE GUN
Eric Allen

Smoke Blackbird had been away too long. The Lequires had seized the Blackbird farm, forcing the Indians and settlers off, and no one seemed willing to fight! He had to fight alone.

THE THIRD RIDER
Barry Cord

Mel Rawlins wasn't going to let anything stand in his way. His father was murdered, his two brothers gone. Now Mel rode for vengeance.

ARIZONA DRIFTERS
W. C. Tuttle

When drifting Dutton and Lonnie Steelman decide to become partners they find that they have a common enemy in the formidable Thurston brothers.

TOMBSTONE
Matt Braun

Wells Fargo paid Luke Starbuck to outgun the silver-thieving stagecoach gang at Tombstone. Before long Luke can see the only thing bearing fruit in this eldorado will be the gallows tree.

HIGH BORDER RIDERS
Lee Floren

Buckshot McKee and Tortilla Joe cut the trail of a border tough who was running Mexican beef into Texas. They stopped the smuggler in his tracks.